COMMENTS BY READERS

"*Matilda* is charming. She provides us with a delightful read," states Anne Somplack, a teacher of reading.

"I have enjoyed *Matilda*. The story was realistic, and I like the way it flowed. I have followed it with the second book, *At The Skylight with Matilda*." Amber Bishop, college student in Ohio.

"*Matilda* is perfectly delightful and so is the second book, *At the Skylight with Matilda*. I highly recommend these books for the young adult." Joan Kaufmann, an avid reader.

"Meet *Matilda*, she is a nanny with character," says Tony Lombardo, news reporter for *The Chronicle Telegram*, Elyria, Ohio.

1st.

Matilda

by Phyllis Levine

Wasteland Press

Shelbyville, KY USA
www.wastelandpress.net

Matilda
By Phyllis Levine

First Printing – 2002
Second Printing – February 2007
Third Printing – August 2011
Fourth Printing – July 2012
ISBN13: 978-1-60047-079-0
illustration by Liquid Library

Library of Congress Control Number: 2007922665

0   1   2   3   4

Other Books by the author:

The Alphabet Beach Song
Small Pleasures (Poetry Book)
At The Skylight with Matilda
Matilda's Way

This book is for Stan the Man. "Let's go."

One

Matilda

Matilda Wiggins stepped out of her old beige Toyota Corolla. Her large brown eyes shone; she had styled her long thick black hair in a ponytail, and the tailored navy suit, pink blouse, and navy shoes she wore complemented her lovely figure.

Matilda tried to dress well for all occasions, and this interview was of the utmost importance, so she knew she had to look her best. Matilda felt proud to have graduated from the English Nanny School in Chagrin Falls, Ohio, and was on her way to meet the Evergreen family.

Her hands trembled as she stared at the colonial house with its bright yellow shutters, yellow door and large bay window. Matilda thought that it looked inviting. Yellow to her was like sunshine. Even so, her stomach churned. She had eaten a small bowl of corn-flakes for breakfast. This was all she could manage, and she wished she could have more confidence like some other women she knew who seemed unafraid to do anything.

She loathed being so reserved, but found it difficult to be asser-tive or authoritative. When she was confident, her voice was as clear as pure spring water, but when nervous, she found herself stuttering and unable to choose the right word. Matilda was homesick for London. She missed her mother and friend Carrie. Carrie's rasping laugh spun through her mind. Matilda remembered Carrie mixing up a joke when she tried to get to the end of it.

Carrie often left funny notes in Matilda's mail box sketched with cartoon characters which she read when she came home from a hard day of waiting on tables with her feet swollen and sore. Lying on her mother's dilapidated old sofa, she would read the latest note. Then her tiredness would disappear. She would roll on the couch and laugh so hard, and reread the note. It was a guarantee that her funny friend could always cheer her up.

There was no phone in her mother's home, no carpeting, no decent furniture; only odd pieces from her mother's family dotted the flat. There was no television, but an old radio on the shelf that sometimes worked, helped keep Matilda informed on what was happening in the world, and if there were a good program on television Matilda wished to see, she would pop over to Carrie's house.

Writing notes and dropping them in Carrie's mailbox was her only way to communicate with her. If she needed to make an important phone call, she would ask a neighbor if it were possible to use the phone.

With all the nothings in her life, Matilda devoured fish and chips, loaded with vinegar, Regents Park with its immaculate lawns, plush pink roses, English voices and the Queen. Yes, she enjoyed all of this. Even though poverty had encumbered Matilda all her life, she was not scarred by it. In fact, she laughed easily and imagined all the great things she might do and become. To her, education was the answer.

Down days sometimes affected her demeanor, but not enough to have her feeling sorry for herself. Matilda did feel concerned about her future, but instead of worrying about it, she decided while very young to work hard. Saving money and giving up little luxuries had not been easy, but a deep determination inside Matilda influenced her to act. This determination to make something of her life was what she decided at an early age. Her imagination was vivid. Surrounded by magazines with pictures of movie stars, television stars, and ordinary people who had become successful, inspired her, so she saved her money for her hopeful trip to America and attend a school there.

Royalty fascinated her. She liked to watch the change of guard at Buckingham Palace, and follow all the news she could read in the media about the Royal family. It was England to her! She was often chastised about her fondness for royalty, but she did not care. She missed it all, but not the small, cold, damp Victorian flat.

Matilda liked dressing in bright colors, but pink was her favorite. Clothed in pink, she felt herself change into a vibrant personality with all shyness gone. She remembered the day her mother had brought home a pink dress with white lace for her seventh birthday. This was her only dress that had not been worn by her older sister Emily. It had a lace bow in the front, and everyone said how pretty she looked in it. When she outgrew the dress, she kept it hidden and would not permit her mother to give it away.

Two

Mrs. Sue Evergreen

Matilda had an inclination to work with children between three and twelve years of age. Information had been available on the family that wished to employ her, and the superintendent advised Matilda to take all her personal belongings with her as the Evergreens would probably hire her as it seemed to be an emergency situation. Mr. Richard Evergreen's wife, Sarah, had died of an aneurysm just two months ago, and the family required a combination nanny and housekeeper immediately, so Matilda prepared herself to do both.

At present, Richard Evergreen's parents were caring for the children, but their plans were to fly to California and not return to Twinsburg for several months. Matilda stood by the front door for a moment admiring the house, finally pressing the bell. A melody chimed which startled her. She glanced at her new Timex watch.

Matilda wasn't late. She was supposed to be at the house by ten, and ten it was. Being on time was important to her. All through her school years she had been told of how one showed one's respect for others by this courtesy. She could still hear Miss Brown's high-pitched voice dictating the virtues of showing up at the appointed time. Miss Brown was quite thin and tall. She had a long face, mousy gray hair that never seemed in place, and her reading glasses often slipped down her nose. Matilda always felt an urge to dash over to her and push them back. Miss Brown's blouse and skirt were creased and looked as though she had slept in them.

Matilda arrived late for class. For the second time that day, her locker would not open. It was plain stuck, and Matilda needed her book for the class, so she arrived five minutes late. Miss Brown frowned when Matilda entered and announced that she would speak to her after class. Cringing, she did not wish to hear Miss Brown's lecture. The worst of the offense was to have the students stare and smirk. Matilda could feel their eyes penetrate and their mumbled insults were heard as they let out an ugly laugh; she bent her head and stared blindly at the desk. Her cheeks burned and the sudden tears smeared her face.

Matilda remembered when she tried out for a part in a school drama and practiced in front of the mirror lines from Romeo and Juliet. In this, she did so well that she was given the role of Lady Capulet. Now she felt she could conquer her shyness. From then on she tried out for other parts. The theater enthralled her; the magic and fantasy gave her courage. When she performed, she could be someone other than herself. It was then confidence reigned.

Inside the house, Mrs. Evergreen, the children's grandmother was clearing dishes off the kitchen table and humming. Richard Evergreen opened the door. "Hi, you must be Matilda Wiggins."

"Yes, that's right."

"Well, we're glad to meet you. Come on in."

Sue Evergreen rushed out of the kitchen. "Oh, it's wonderful that you're here!" She fluttered around Matilda. "Let me take your coat and purse. I'll put everything in the closet. Can I get you something to drink? Would you like some coffee or tea?"

"No thank you, nothing right now, Mrs. Evergreen."

Matilda tried her best to act and look confident, but words she tried to say would not come, and on top of that she had almost tripped over the Oriental rug in the hall. "Oh my, they will think I am careless and clumsy," thought Matilda.

On the contrary, Sue was delighted with the appearance of this beautiful English girl. The superintendent of the school had sent others to be interviewed, but Sue had not found one she thought suitable, but Matilda impressed her immediately. For one thing, she did not have a tattoo plastered on her arms or face or a ring on the tip of her tongue. "Yes, this girl is the right one. I'll call the superintendent of the school to let her know that Matilda is it." These thoughts entered Sue's mind as she continued to look over Matilda.

Sue could not fathom the fashion of teens and young adults. Not that she cared. She just did not understand the extreme they went to in decorating and mutilating their bodies or dying their hair purple, or the makeup that made their faces look like vampires. "It's that rotten music they listen to and TV that's messed them up," thought Sue.

Sue's green eyes were like a cat's. She noticed the smallest detail, and seemed to scrutinize others' thoughts. All her emotions showed on her face. "This generation has no manners. It must be all those single mothers raising children alone with no father in the home that has messed them up. They have never learned etiquette. What a shame."

Richard often heard these complaints about the younger generation. Nothing could convince his mother that this was just a stage they were going through.

As Sue busied herself in the house, she sang at the top of her voice. Lyrics to most of the old songs were stored in her head like a computer, and she would burst out the words with clarity and accuracy as she worked. Old band music, the giants of the early forties and fifties boomed from the stereo.

Sue took good care of herself. She looked younger than her age. Her blonde short haircut and painted nails stood out like weapons, and her figure was as trim as a young woman. Growing old was not in her vocabulary, so she decided to stay in shape by watching what she ate. Sue put old age aside, and told her grandchildren that she was Nana, and definitely not to call her Grandmother.

"Welcome Matilda, we are pleased to have you here. You are our nanny. The children are upstairs in the playroom. I'll call them down soon." She shook Matilda's hand.

"Let me help you get your luggage out of your car," said Richard. Matilda gave him her car keys. He returned and placed the suitcase in the hall. Matilda handed over important papers to Richard. They included a copy of her diploma, her license, and a record that stated it was legal for her to be in the United States.

"Can I keep these?" asked Richard.

"Why, yes."

Richard examined them. "Well, everything seems to be in order. Thanks, Matilda." The phone rang, and he dashed to answer it.

Three

Joey and Jennie

Matilda picked up her case and asked if there were someplace she could put it. "Oh, we'll take it up to your room later." Sue called out. "Joey, Jennifer, come on down. I have someone you should meet."

"Well, my dear, you do know that my husband and I have a florist shop in California and we must leave in three days. It has been such an ordeal, here, and I do hate to leave my precious grandchildren, but if we do not go, I'm afraid we would lose the shop which has taken a while to establish. It is almost fall, and the Christmas season will be here soon enough. Our florist shop is in good hands, but we have so many things to arrange." Sue glanced out of the picture window.

"Some of the leaves are changing. I just love the lushness of fall. In the middle of October, you will find the woods and parks at the height of the season. The colors then are breathtaking. I won't be here to see it, but you enjoy it." Sue gazed out of the large picture window.

Matilda thought of her first year in Chagrin Falls, which was spent studying and not much time for nature. In London, she did not notice many trees unless she went to the local park, but most Londoners had gardens in the back of their houses where a variety of flowers bloomed, and in June, bunches of red roses flourished in the fronts of homes. Matilda adored roses. Now, she would look forward to the autumn in Ohio. Matilda preferred to say "autumn." The word sounded so much richer.

"The children are so little. Joey is six and Jennie four. It has been very hard on all of us. Even now, I'm afraid to leave them. You do understand dear, don't you?" Sue's eyes filled with tears. "My dear, please, excuse me. I am trying to do better." Sue continued to chat and blow her nose.

"Their mother, Sarah was so young; just thirty years old when she died, and what a way she had with the children. She just took them everywhere. Nothing seemed to stop her. She planned activities and played all sorts of games with them. Oh my, I don't know how she did it. She was just so impish and creative. I'll never get over it. Look around. The house is simply filled with her artwork. Oh dear, I'm just getting carried away. Now, what was I saying?" Sue attempted to get herself in control.

Matilda glanced at the walls which were filled with modern art. Matilda did not understand much about art, but knew the paintings were unusual and could see that Sarah must have been quite talented.

Richard strolled into the kitchen "Well, I see that my mother is explaining how to take care of the children. Don't over do it Mom. Matilda will catch on, I'm sure. It looks as though I have to get to the office. They are having some problems with the new computers that came in." Richard grabbed his jacket. "I'll see you all later." He knew his mother would handle everything.

"Children, Joey, Jennie, didn't you hear me? Come on down here, now!" Mrs. Evergreen composed herself. She had dried her eyes and placed the dishes in the sink and turned on the hot water faucet.

Joey and Jennie appeared at the kitchen door. Jennie held her teddy bear with one ear missing. Joey played with a rubber band.

"Come here and give your Nana a hug. There now, I want you to meet Matilda."

The two children stared at her. Joey reached in his pocket and shot a rubber band across the room just missing Matilda's ear.

"Now, Joey, rubber bands can be dangerous. Don't do that again." Joey shrugged his shoulders and scowled at his grandmother.

Matilda offered her hand to them. "Glad to meet you both."

She thought how sweet they looked. "I'm Matilda. I'm going to be your nanny."

"What's a nanny?" asked Joey.

"A nanny takes care of children."

"We don't need care. You have a funny name."

"Now, Joey that wasn't polite. Well, dear, I think your name sounds musical to me." Sue was getting anxious and beginning to lose her patience.

Sue put her finger to her mouth to hush her grandchildren while she spoke to Matilda. Joey made loud snorting noises and whistled like a train while circling Matilda.

"Joey, stop that at once." Sue grabbed Joey and sat him next to her. Jennie sat on the floor quietly listening.

"How did your parents choose your name?" asked Sue.

"My mother liked listening to recordings of Harry Belafonte. His style and rhythm appealed to her. Belafonte recorded the song "Matilda," and she liked it, so that's how I got my name. Singers of the fifties and sixties are my mother's favorites. She listens to Frank Sinatra, Sammy Davis Jr, Dinah Shore, Dean Martin and Louis Armstrong. Oh, there were so many others. Why, I could fill a whole book. She likes ballads with a melody, but the music I like has not thrilled her at all. When I tell people my name, they don't forget it. If it's easier, the children can call me Mattie."

"I think they will like that," replied Sue. "Your mother and I have something in common. They don't write the music with good lyrics or sweet melodies. It's just garbage these days and it hurts your ears. Thank goodness for the old recordings." Sue beamed and her green eyes grew as large as an owl's.

"It would be nice to meet Matilda's mother. They could talk about the old days," thought Sue. For a moment, Sue had a faraway look in her eyes. She could visualize dancing to Tommy Dorsey's band or even Glenn Miller. Although they were a little before her time, their sounds lingered in her mind.

"Let's help Matilda with her luggage. "Do you think you are ready to take on my two grandchildren?"

"Yes, I am."

"Joey, see if you can pick up her case, and Jennie can come help show where her room is."

"Oh, thank you." said Matilda.

"Here, Joey you take up my bag, and I'll carry the suitcase." Matilda glanced at Joey, but he was engrossed in his game and ignored the request and ran up the stairs.

"Joey, you come back here," beckoned Sue. Joey refused. He flew to his room shooting rubber bands through the air. He found them in the kitchen drawer ready to aim at Matilda. A door slammed. Matilda held her breath and ears as she felt them pop. Sue caught up with Joey and made him sit in his room for a time out.

Four

Matilda Adjusts

Matilda liked the room with the flowered wallpaper and bed-spread that matched. She unpacked her suitcase and placed her clothes neatly in the antique chest. "Joey needs lots of encouragement," thought Matilda with a sigh. She left the room and entered the playroom. With Joey's time out over, both children were playing with building blocks.

"Hello, there. Is that a fun game?" asked Matilda.

Jennie smiled, but Joey did not look up. Matilda waited for a response, but there was none. Downstairs she could hear the radio and the weatherman announce the temperature for the day. He joked about his birthday. Matilda thought of hers which was not far off. On December 9, she would be twenty-two.

The Evergreen house was new. It had a long staircase in the center, high ceilings, oversized windows and plenty of space to get lost. Matilda joined Sue who was rinsing the breakfast dishes.

"Just a minute dear, I'll give you the grand tour, and here is a list of names that you will need. I've included the children's doctor, dentist, a close neighbor and the children's friends. I think I've covered everything."

"Thanks. Do you have a bulletin board?"

"Yes. It's right next to the phone."

"I'll put it there."

"Well, what do you think?" Sue asked.

"I'm a little bewildered but I'm sure I'll find everything." Matilda knew she would be in a state of confusion for a few days. She'd already opened the wrong doors. Her sense of direction was not the best.

"By the way, the cleaning lady will come on Wednesday. Richard writes her a check. Make sure you remind him. He is so preoccupied. His business keeps him hopping. Poor man, he is a single father now which is the last thing he or any of us expected. Single women having children and no husband always upset him. Now, he is in the same situation. Oh, I was speaking about the cleaning lady. Oh dear, I have too much on my mind. She's Mrs. Miller. I don't know why they had to build such a big house. I just hope Richard can keep it up. It seems these days the newer houses are so large. Well, dear, I suppose that's what they wanted. I'm glad you came on a Saturday. We do appreciate it."

"I believe the superintendent of the Chagrin Nanny School told you the working arrangements. Anyway, I'll go over them. Weekends are your days off, and of course you know that you will be paid a bonus for doing the light housework and cooking. We are grateful that you agreed to help Richard run the household. I don't believe he knows where anything is. I should have shown him when he was young the importance of running a house. I believe there are courses in high school for both sexes. I think that's a great thing. Oh well, it's too late to train him. I'm afraid I've spoiled Richard. He's absolutely useless around the house. I don't think he can make coffee. Of course, he will cut the grass and paint when necessary, but that's it. Sue threw her hands in the air and shook her head in dismay. Can you can cook a little?"

Matilda could manage to do a little cooking, but it was not one of her favorite things.

"I do a have a few menus I can put together. Nutrition was important in our courses."

"Oh that's fine, dear. Richard has arrangements for a baby sitter. Linda Hayes lives down the street. She will come here on the weekends. Here is her phone number. I'll put it on the board and in the address book. You can't afford to lose it. Is there anything you need to ask me?"

"Not right now, Mrs. Evergreen, but I'm sure there will be something I'll need to know."

Matilda thanked her for the information. She was so excited to be in the States with all the space and beautiful homes. "This house could make three in London," she thought to herself. Living in a glamorous home thrilled her even if it was only for a while.

"What do you think of the house?"

"It's just lovely, Mrs. Evergreen." Matilda thought of the queen in England, and what it must be like living in a palace. To her, this mansion was one. She could not imagine rooms that were as large as this house, or anywhere else, except in a palace, or in those immense estates that she had seen in the English countryside. On a bus tour, she had visited castles and couldn't believe that people lived in them through the centuries. Now the upkeep was very high, so the owners had made them tourist attractions to help maintain them.

"Matilda, tell me about your self. Where were you born?" asked Sue.

"In London, I've lived there all my life. My parents divorced when I was young, and I have an older sister Emily, and a brother Eric. I stayed with my mother, and my father visited occasionally, and we'd go out for dinner. I'm the youngest." Matilda quickly changed the subject.

"I've spent many nights reading and studying the United States, and made up my mind when I was quite young that I would come here."

Matilda made sure she divulged nothing about her father. His drunken binges still haunted her and filled her with horror. When he was sober, he was gentle with the whole family. For years, she had done her best to overcome the memories of the harrowing fights between her parents. It was her mother who kept the family together. Her father was an embarrassment that she would not discuss with anyone. She often dreamed of what it would have been like to have a father take her places and tell her she was pretty.

At six years of age, her mother threw her father out. Not hearing the loud voices in the night, the screaming, and objects flying calmed her. During her early years, she could not concentrate at school, and at times was scared to go home. Her unhappy childhood influenced her need to care for children. In no way could she tell Sue Evergreen about her father or her early years. She had buried it all long ago.

A man of about fifty five opened the front door.

Richard's father had returned from a game of golf.

"Hi, am I missing anything? What a super game. Boy, it was just great!" He slid the golf clubs into the hall closet.

"Who do we have here?"

Sue jumped up. "Al, this is Matilda Wiggins, our English nanny."

"Well, you are just what the doctor ordered. You're a good looking chick."

"Al, that's no way to talk."

"Okay, don't get bent out of shape, but she sure looks like someone needed around here. Sue, I'm half starved. What's for lunch?"

"What would you like?" asked Matilda.

"Just call me Al, and my wife's name is Sue. Remember to call her that."

"Fine, I'll try to do that."

Sue Evergreen rolled her eyes in surprise. "Matilda, I'll show you where everything is and we'll put something together."

Five

So Long for Now

Matilda set to work in a kitchen that she would learn to know. She felt her courage return and her repetitive shyness vanish. In her heart, she knew she could accomplish anything. The three days passed quickly and the Evergreens were ready to fly to California.

"Now," said Al. "You take care, young lady, and Sue and I will keep in touch." He gave Matilda a wink and a pat on the back. Matilda smiled and told them to have a safe flight to California.

Richard set out to the driveway to warm his car and waited to take his parents to the Cleveland Hopkins Airport.

"If I've forgotten anything, Richard, just mail it, dear. Now, you two, give us a big kiss. It has to last till our next visit, so I need a big one!" Jennie held on to her grandmother.

Al gave Joey a bear hug. "Say, Joey, practice that swing. When I come back, we'll play a round, okay?"

Joey turned to run in the house.

"Joey," called Richard. "Come back here! Now, say 'bye to your grandparents properly."

Joey pouted for an instant, pulled a face, and then begrudgingly kissed them.

"Be good. See you soon. Love you," Sue called out.

Sue was confident she chose Matilda, and was responsible for her salary, and told Richard she would mail a check each month. Richard had balked at first, but Sue reminded him that a nanny was a big need right now, and felt it her duty to help him.

Running a new business would be difficult enough. She worried that her grandchildren would end up in a foster home, and this nagging thought hammered in her mind. She knew she would not sleep if they were placed there. This was the best choice if Richard would not permit the children to live with her.

Six

Concerns about
Joey and Jennie

Matilda found the house ghostly quiet without the Evergreens. Matilda was concerned about Joey, but knew she could sort it all out. Monday, she would take him to school.

It was such a short distance that she decided to walk to Joey's school to bring him home. Jennie came along. She put on her new red coat and hat. As Matilda strolled, she thought of Sue Evergreen and what she had said about autumn. Some of the trees' leaves were changing their colors. Matilda wished she could paint and capture the scene.

"How did Joey do in school today?" Richard put his keys on top of the desk in the kitchen.

"It went well, Mr. Evergreen."

"Call me Richard. There's no formality around here, Matilda."

"Oh, I'll try to remember that."

Matilda thought of the differences in England. Here people liked to be called by their first names. To her, it did not seem respectful, especially when speaking to people who were older than she. She did not want to insult anyone, so she decided to ask what was considered proper. Politeness and good manners were important to her.

She knew she had to learn to speak American English. At the school, she had a list of words that she studied. Some students told her that she should learn to translate her English sayings into American. Matilda kept saying tap instead of faucet and lift instead of elevator and dozens of other words that confused others who spoke to her. Constantly she reminded herself to use American English. People often gave her a puzzled look when she used London expressions.

Waking Joey to get him off to school was like fighting a bull. Matilda set the alarm for seven thirty a.m. School began at nine. The night before she gathered Joey's clothes and placed them on his chair by his bed, but instead of dressing he played games. Like a turtle, he was unprepared to move. Matilda tried to persuade Joey to dress, but he refused, so she ended up dressing him.

Tuesday, Joey said he felt sick, but seemed fine on Monday. Matilda took his temperature. It was normal. He complained of a cramp in his right leg, so Matilda massaged it. There was nothing wrong. She hurried Joey into the bathroom to get ready for school and waited in the hall, checking her watch constantly.

"I'll be out in a minute!"

Matilda knocked on the bathroom door calling on him to come out. Richard heard the commotion and threw the door open. Joey had not dressed. He had filled the tub with water and was playing with his boats. Richard was furious and scolded him, telling him all privileges were gone for the next two days. Joey shrugged his shoulders and yelled, "I don't care, and you're a stupid idiot."

"Did you hear that? Where is he getting all this from?" Richard clenched his fists.

The following morning, Joey dressed and washed quickly and asked Matilda in a whispery voice why his mother had died, and was she still angry over his muddy shoes. Matilda sat with him and said that his mother had very bad pains in her head, and they were so bad that nothing could help. She convinced Joey that his mother was not angry at anything.

Joey listened and seemed to accept this. Then he asked if he was going to die from a headache too. Matilda held him close, and said, "Of course not, Joey."

On Wednesday, Mrs. Miller came to clean the house. She was in her fifties and worked for two others in the neighborhood. She was proud of the way she cleaned, and announced, "I don't mop floors. I scrub 'em. These young people have no idea how to clean a house, and them ads on the TV tell 'em to use that fancy stuff, and just mop."

"I tell you Miss. Matilda. They got it all wrong. You got to gets in the corners, and gets down on hands and knees and give 'em floors a scrub. With kids and the dirt they track in and gum on the floor, it ain't right to mop."

"Ain't that so?" Mrs. Miller misplaced her glasses. "Now where did I put 'em." Matilda found them on the kitchen counter on top of the radio.

"Oh, that sweet Sarah, she was such a lady! Ain't many like her. And pretty as a picture, she was, and always fussing over her Joey, and she dressed Jennie like a princess too. Life ain't fair."

On the piano sat Sarah's photograph. Mrs. Miller carefully dusted it. The photo was recent. Large luminous blue eyes gazed out; long red hair framed her face. Sarah had given it to Richard the year before on Valentine's Day.

"They got this house and worried if I'd come back. They didn't have to worry. I told 'em, I'd do it. It ain't that bad! And now she's gone. It's awful. Ain't it just awful? Well I'll finish up, Matilda." Mrs. Miller stepped out on the porch.

"I've got to have a smoke. I know I shouldn't, but I've tried everything to stop. It don't work."

"Thanks for the good job, Mrs. Miller. The house and floors smell fresh and look so nice."

She handed her the check. Matilda and Jennie waved as she climbed into her old green Ford Escort. The muffler was heard grunting way down the street.

"Looks like Mrs. Miller could do with a new car. I hope she makes it home." Matilda felt sorry for her and knew she was struggling to survive. She gave her some old gloves and a wool hat. "The weather would be cold soon," thought Matilda.

After dinner, Joey pleaded to play with his friend, Steve, but Richard reminded him that he had lost his privileges. Joey ran screaming to his room, and threw his mother's Bible across the floor. Sarah had often read psalms and Bible stories at bedtime. Joey had kept it at his bedside. Matilda jumped at the noise.

"No Matilda, he will be all right. He has to learn to behave. "Damn." Richard hit his fist on the kitchen table. "Excuse me." He apologized and stalked off to his office where his papers awaited.

The rest of the evening was quiet. Matilda washed the dinner dishes and gave Jennie a bath. Matilda tucked Jennie in bed. Then tip-toed into Joey's room. He was curled up asleep with his clothes and shoes on with the light blaring in his face. Matilda untied his shoes and slipped them off, pulled a blanket up to his neck and gently kissed his forehead. She saw the Bible on the floor and picked it up and placed in on the bedside table. Quietly, she switched off the light and closed the door.

Seven

Matilda Goes on a Spree

One cold Saturday, Matilda drove to the Randall Mall. Splurging on something pretty was what she felt like doing. She hadn't spent any money on herself in months. Nearly all of her salary went into the bank for her education. A pink dress caught her attention. The color pink had become her weakness. When she saw the dress on a mannequin, she knew she had to own it, so she selected the accessories to match. She had not focused on a day when to wear the outfit, but did not care. This was the first time in her life she had spent so much money on herself.

As a waitress, her salary never went far. Nevertheless, Matilda saved a portion each week for her intended trip to the States. She could not borrow any money or ask her father for help. When he found a job, it never lasted because of his lateness and arguments with his bosses, so Matilda could not ask for any assistance. She felt it best to not bother him.

Matilda and her mother worked as waitresses in a busy restaurant in the West End of London, and the tips were quite decent. Suddenly, Matilda felt guilty and knew she should have sent some of her earnings home.

As she shopped, the sales people commented about her accent, and asked: "Are you from London? Have you seen the queen?" Then she knew how much her English accent stood out, but she was not about to change it.

Matilda stopped at Wendy's and ordered a salad. The teens paraded by, and she stared at their baggy pants, greased hair, and earphones. Their boldness stood out, and she felt intimidated because they looked like a gang, but soon realized that teens liked to look and dress alike. It set them apart from the adults, and were more than likely harmless. Nevertheless, she was fascinated.

She recalled Mrs. Evergreen's remarks, and now she saw for herself. She ate her salad, and tried not to stare, and concentrated on the shoppers and daydreamed about her future.

Matilda thought of the places she wished to tour and hoped they resembled the articles she read in books. After all, she had spent many months in the library studying the touring spots of America. Where she would travel, depended on money she could earn. She thought of her mother and wondered when she would have enough money to travel home. She worried if her mother was feeling well, and if her cat, Nifty, was missing her. He often followed her to the bus stop, and she would carry him home. People often said cats were independent. Nifty did not seem like that. She brushed his black and white fur to make his coat shine, and right now, she wanted to stroke him and hear his purr. She glanced at her watch and decided to go back to the house.

"Matilda, have you ever seen an American football game on TV?" asked Richard. Matilda closed the front door. "No I haven't."

"Next Saturday I have tickets for a game. The Cleveland Browns are playing against the New York Giants. I'm taking Joey. Would you like to go? Do you have anything planned?"

"No not yet. I don't know anything about football." She remembered her brother and the crises he went through when his favorite soccer team lost. He would sulk like a baby, and she could not fathom why people became so upset when their team lost.

"That's all right. Joey and I will teach you." Richard thought it was time to show Matilda one of America's favorite past times. "You come, okay?" Matilda thought it best to say yes.

Eight

Matilda feels Spoiled

Matilda opened her packages and laid the pink dress, hat, shoes, and bow on her bed. She slipped off her clothes and put on the dress, and tuned the radio to Magic 105.7. The door opened; a small voice called: "Mattie."

"Hi Jennie, what have you been up to today?"

"Come here." Matilda held Jennie's little hands and together they rollicked about the room. Jennie tried on Matilda's new hat and swayed to the music of rock 'n' roll.

"Okay Jennie, I need to take these new clothes off and put them away for a special day." Jennie gave Matilda her hat and together they went downstairs giggling.

"What's a special day?"

"I don't know yet, but you are a special girl!"

"When's Mommy coming home?" Matilda sat down on the stairs and held Jennie.

"Jennie, your Mommy loves you, but she can't come home. She is in a happy place, and she wants you to be happy too."

"Oh. Let's go see Linda. She played with me all day and she's going home."

The phone rang. Richard answered it.

"Well hi, how are all of you doing?"

"What's that? You are expecting us to come for Hanukkah and Christmas combined." Richard hesitated and a frown swept over his face.

"Well I haven't made up my mind, yet. Considering the circumstances, I thought I'd stay put. Yes, I know we usually come, but this year I wasn't sure what our plans would be. You want to talk to Matilda?" Richard handed Matilda the phone.

"It's my mother-in-law; she would like to speak to you."

"Hello, Matilda. I've been told you are from England. How wonderful. How are the children? I'm so looking forward to meeting you. Thank you for caring for our grandchildren."

Matilda could not think of anything relevant to say, but knew she wanted to discuss Joey, but said nothing about his welfare.

"I hope to see you during the Hanukkah and Christmas season. Richard and Sarah usually came down then. Without Sarah, it's hard for all of us, but I would like this tradition to continue. Would you like to join the family?" Janet Rosen waited for an answer. Matilda thought of the sun, palm trees, and sand.

"It sounds wonderful." Matilda had always wanted to visit Florida. She had heard so much about it.

Matilda handed the phone to Richard. He gave his mother-in-law all the latest news and left the invitation on hold.

Nine

Joey's Problem

Ron and Janet Rosen lived in Miami and owned a first class hotel named the Skylight Inn. It was on the beach. Their son Mark, an accountant, worked with them, and their other two sons, Jacob and Aaron were finishing up graduate school.

Sarah, their only daughter had attended Ohio State where she had met Richard in one of their classes. She sat next to him, and fumbled in her purse for a pen but could not locate it. Then remembered she had left her pens in the dormitory. She had been in a hurry to get to class. Richard, who was in the next seat, supplied a pencil. He became spellbound when he looked at her. Her smile and red hair captivated him.

They married after graduating from the university. Richard was of the Christian faith and Sarah Jewish. Both families accepted each others' religion and held a family reunion every summer in Twinsburg, Ohio. They selected August so they could see the twins who come from all over the country to the festival.

"Before you know it December will be here, Matilda. How are you getting along? How's Joey behaving? My mother told the school that having a nanny from London would be a good experience for the children, and I feel that is true. You seem to be managing well. What do you think, Matilda?" Richard looked at Matilda with gratitude.

Matilda smiled at what Richard had said to her. Compliments were never easy for her to accept. Finally, she answered that she was pleased that it was working out, and to herself she had to admit that she was much more confident at being a nanny. Everyone treated her with respect and this added to her feeling good about herself.

"Is there anything you need or want to share with me?"

Matilda blurted, "Joey worries me. He is so sad and moody at times. I'm not always sure what to do."

"Yes, I know. I have made an appointment with a child's counselor after school on Monday. Joey was very close to his mother, and Jennie wants to know when her mother is coming home. I am lost on what to tell them. I try to explain in the best way I can. As for Joey, I can't make him understand that his mother is dead. I've decided to take the children to Florida on Christmas break. Everything seems to be going smoothly in my business. The Skylight Inn is great. Do you want to join us?" Richard was thinking about Matilda's friends who she had met at the English Nanny School. They occasionally phoned her. Perhaps she would like to be with them during the holidays, but Matilda said she was eager to see Florida.

"We celebrate Jewish and Christian holy days. Hanukkah does not always come exactly around Christmas, but we acknowledge them at the same time. Jennie is just beginning to understand the festivities, and Joey likes getting a present for the eight days. Sarah taught the story of lights to him. Seeing his other grandparents will be good for him and Jennie. It's good that you want to come with us."

Ten

Football and Autumn

November arrived in a blaze of color. The trees filled the streets, shimmering with red and yellow leaves that transformed the dark cloudy day. Leaves were scattered throughout the yard. They stuck on shoes, and blew in the house when the front door opened. Matilda raked the dry leaves to the sidewalk while Jennie squealed as she ran through the thick piles. "Jennie, if you keep doing that, we'll never get all the leaves into the street." Matilda knew the fun that Jennie was having and so was she.

Jennie had grown close to Matilda. She showed Jennie how to do water color pictures, puzzles, and read picture books. Matilda often invited Courtney to play with Jennie. Courtney lived one block from the house and was close in age to Jennie. Her mother had been Sarah's friend and good neighbor.

"Matilda, are you ready? Looks like a great day for the game. We have to leave early, so we can get a parking place. I have a Brown's hat and jacket you can wear."

Richard was pacing the hall and wondered why it took women so long to get ready to go out. Matilda finally appeared looking like a fan and anxious to see her first football game.

"Linda there's a note on the bulletin board for Jennie's schedule." Matilda had everything organized for her. Joey ran up the stairs then sailed down the banisters.

"Hey, that's enough of that," yelled Richard.

"I'm wondering how we ever got along without you, Matilda." She smiled. Matilda enjoyed her job and was determined to help Joey through his trauma.

Matilda commented at the size of the Cleveland Browns' stadium. Watching the people in their Browns' costumes and the loud comments from the crowd had Matilda laughing throughout the game. When the team lost, the crowd booed.

"It's a new team. They have to grow," commented Richard, "but they will get better." Joey jumped all over his seat and hollered along with the crowd. Richard patted his head and explained the strategies of the game.

"So, what do you think of football?"

"I liked the hotdogs and fans, but I'll have to learn the game."

"You do that, Matilda."

"Thank you for inviting me."

"My pleasure," answered Richard.

Most of the autumn leaves had disappeared. Morning frost covered the grass, and winter's chill had crept in. Matilda made Joey wear his heavy jacket, and drove him to school because of his slowness in getting ready. Matilda found herself scowling and her voice rising when she tried to get him to move faster. Taking a deep breath and counting to ten helped her not to lose her self-control. She wondered if Joey would ever improve.

No complaints were heard from Joey's kindergarten teacher, but Matilda decided to inquire how he was getting along. She left a message with the school secretary for Joey's teacher to call. Matilda straightened the kitchen and put a load of clothes in the washing machine. The phone rang.

"This is the Evergreen Residence."

"Hello, my dear. How nice to hear your voice. How was your Thanksgiving? Did you work hard? How did the flowers look on the dining room table?"

"Oh, didn't Richard call you?"

"No, he didn't, dear."

"I'm sorry he didn't. The yellow roses were gorgeous."

"Oh, that's good. Yellow was Sarah's favorite color, but you probably noticed it throughout the house. That's Richard, for you. He's busy with the new computers and his business. Forgets his mother, but I forgive him! I'll have to reach him on the Internet, but I really prefer to talk to him. Tell him to teach Joey the Internet as soon as he learns to write. I need to communicate to at least one member of my family!"

"These days, everyone is on the Internet, but me. I am plain old fashioned. I still like to hear the person's voice. I just like to gab, I guess. Are you keeping well, Matilda? "

"I'm fine except for an occasional cold."

"Matilda, don't you get sick. The whole family needs you. Now what was it I need to ask you? I'm trying to remember. Oh, I know. What did you cook for Thanksgiving?"

Matilda laughed as she explained her nervousness when she roasted her first turkey, but was glad that Richard had told her the story of the Pilgrims. "I'm learning something new everyday."

"That's good. Well dear, I have to get busy. Lots of orders are coming in. Bye, give the children kisses from Nana."

Matilda liked hearing from Sue Evergreen. Even though she had only known her for three days, she felt her warmth, and she always seemed to be in a good mood and have something pleasant to say to her.

Matilda brought in the mail and placed it on the desk. There was no mail for her yet. She looked out the bay window and saw a neighbor walking his golden retriever.

"I bet the children would like a pet. I know I would. A black cat would be just the thing for the family."

Eleven

A Talk with Mrs. Adams

The next morning, Matilda received a phone message from Joey's teacher for a meeting on Wednesday morning. She said nothing about it to Richard. She thought she would find out what was going on in school first.

Richard had taken Joey for an evaluation and said the counselor gave him several ways to work with him, and to bring in Jennie if she needed some guidance. Richard knew he had not confronted Sarah's death, and Joey needed to talk about it.

"I have been too busy with my new company. Even though my parents were here, I should have spent more time with him. I am taking off early, and I'll pick Joey up after school and play a little football at the park."

"That's great. Joey will love it," said Matilda. She was pleased that Richard was finally going to give his children more time.

Since Thanksgiving, little snow had fallen. Now it fell like thick puffs of fine sugar, coating streets and walkways. Houses and rooftops began to look like an old fashioned Christmas card.

Matilda stood in wonder. It often rained in London, and what snow they had was often soggy. Most days were dismal and dark. An umbrella accompanied Matilda in preparation for drizzle and heavy rain, but here she was in the midst of a snowstorm and played like a little child. She threw snowballs at a Maple tree, chased the children, and had them screaming at the top of their lungs. Although the temperature was freezing, it was a dry snow. Matilda felt warm and exhilarated on this frigid day.

Wednesday, Mrs. Miller came. Matilda and Jennie left for Joey's school. Matilda sat across from Mrs. Adam's desk which was full of artwork, scissors, paste, and photos of children staring up under a glass top. Around the room were posters and letters of the alphabet.

"What a pretty room!"

"Thank you. Glad you like it."

"The reason I'm here is to gather information on Joey's behavior, and I appreciate your time to meet me."

"Welcome to kindergarten. Tell me, are you a family member?"

"No, I'm here on behalf of his father. He is at his business. I'm Joey's nanny. I'm Matilda Wiggins."

"Oh, I see. That's fine."

Mrs. Adams looked through her record book. She wore a bright red dress which matched her welcoming rosy lips and smile. Everything about her indicated that she liked her job, and was prepared to listen. She looked through her notes.

"At times he is very quiet, and does not want to join in an activity, and at others, he is so active and laughs when I wish him to listen. Often, he disrupts the other children, and wants the toy they are using. Lately, he doesn't like to share."

"Sometimes, he has this blank stare. Yes. I do see a problem. He doesn't seem interested in doing much of anything which is getting to be a frequent habit. Is there something I should know?"

"Yes, Mrs. Adams, his mother died two months ago. Joey's grieving."

"I am truly sorry. It must be dreadful for him." She wrote the information in her book and offered her condolences.

"Let me see, there are ways you can work with him to help through this crisis. Have him draw pictures of his mother and talk about the good times he had with her. In fact, the more you talk to him about her, the better it will be for Joey. Be assured I shall do all I can to work him through this."

Mrs. Adams shook Matilda's hand and patted it. "I will do my best to report to you any change."

"Thank you, I'm glad to have met you." Matilda was relieved that Joey's teacher knew the reason for his bad behavior, and most of all she promised to help.

That evening, Matilda told Richard of her meeting with Mrs. Adams and Joey's disruptive behavior in school. Richard listened with a look of forlorn.

"I'm glad you went to see his teacher. This news is not good." Richard sat quietly, listened and felt anxious. He thought of how his life had dramatically changed in just a few months and how he fumbled through each day, not sure in which direction to go. He found his voice.

"It seems I'm away too many hours. I will make a good effort to come home early tomorrow and take the children down to the park. There's a steep hill where they can play with their sled. Thanks for going to see his teacher, Matilda, but I'm the one who should have gone."

He took of his tie and jacket, slumped down in his brown leather armchair, and closed his eyes to think.

"Well, with the counselor and the teacher recommendations, we should be able to help Joey get through Sarah's death." He sat a while staring into space. "Thanks again, Matilda. I plan to change a lot of things."

Twelve

Snow and Matilda

Matilda opened the mailbox and brought the mail in. Several letters were addressed to her. Opening her birthday cards brought a smile to her face. Many were from England. She adored the pretty verses and illustrations, which she reread several times. Matilda liked the way the cards brightened the kitchen, and stuck them on the refrigerator. She was pleased that her family and friends had remembered her birthday. It made her feel close to them.

Matilda sang as she wiped off coffee stains and crumbs off the kitchen counters. Jennie came in and asked if they were having a party and birthday cake.

"No, I don't believe we are. When you are a big five, we'll celebrate and have your favorite cake that you can help decorate." Jennie thought that sounded fine.

"I'm going to color a picture for you," and off she went to find her crayons.

When Richard put his brief case on his desk he looked at the refrigerator. "Why Matilda, it's your birthday and you never said a word! Come on. Let's all go out to dinner and celebrate. If the snow keeps up, I'll take the children sledding tomorrow, but for this evening, it'll be dinner, chocolate cake and ice cream for Matilda. Come on let's go."

A foot of snow fell during the night. It nestled around the house and blocked doorways and covered window ledges. The news announcer said there would be no school. Joey shrieked with joy. .He got out a shovel and tried to clear the heavy snow.

"Are we going to the park like Dad promised?" asked Joey.

"Your dad is coming home early and we are going sledding."

"Great. Can I play with my sled now?"

"Let's get it out of the garage." Richard drove up as Matilda struggled to pull the shed off the top shelf.

"Dad, Dad!"

Richard waved and got out of his car. Matilda was glad Richard had kept his word. Joey ran to greet his father and was met with a big hug.

It was the second day the schools closed. Opening the blind, Joey stared at the thick snow, and ran downstairs two at a time yelling, "Snow, snow! Where's my dad?"

Joey rushed out to the voice of Matilda calling him back to eat his breakfast. It was useless. Her calls faded as Joey rolled in the snow. Richard dug into a large icy chunk, and lifted it to the side of the driveway. He welcomed his little son who wished to help.

Snowplows were at work in driveways, and shovels were kept busy all morning. Richard managed to get out and go to work after cleaning the driveway for the second time in just a few hours.

The three finished molding a snowman and topped its head with an old hat. Matilda took a photograph.

"Frosty here looks great. This is a day to remember. I'm snowbound on my first winter in Ohio." Joey and Jennie marched around their snowman, happy as two penguins in the icy arctic.

Matilda noticed a gradual change in Joey. His tantrums and moods were not as bad. She had spent time talking to him about his mother. Joey drew pictures of his family. It was reassurance that Joey required and this his nanny gave. Matilda was pleased that she had listened to what Mrs. Adams had suggested she do. As for Jennie, she seemed fine, but Matilda was still concerned, and kept a keen eye on her.

Thirteen

Matilda's Decision

Richard hung up the phone. "Well it's all set. We are off to Florida on December twenty second." He picked up Jennie and embraced her. In just two weeks we shall see your Grandma and Grandpa Rosen. How does that sound?"

"Matilda, let me know if the children need clothes for the trip. I haven't a clue about sizes, or what to buy, and you will need some lighter weight clothes. As you probably know, it's hot in Florida. Here is my charge card. Use your judgment on prices. Check the sales." Matilda was surprised that Richard gave her such complete trust.

Richard was concerned about Matilda meeting people in her age group, and mentioned this to her, but she just was not interested. He was thankful and glad she was dedicated to his children.

Matilda was in no hurry to join a social club. Her first priority was caring for the children. She wanted to do especially well on her first job. Eventually, she would go out to meet others and learn about the American culture. Matilda had broken off a relationship with her boyfriend in London. John More was angry at her decision to leave for the States, and said it was an overrated country and full of violence. He believed she would be unsafe. John had said England is the best place on earth, and how could she possibly leave.

John wanted her to marry him, but Matilda said no. She enjoyed his company, but considered him only a friend.

"No John," she had said. "I want see for myself what the States are like while I'm young. Don't believe everything you read in newspapers." He had been flabbergasted. This was a Matilda he did not recognize. Nevertheless, he continued to pursue her.

Defiantly, Matilda stood at the front door and looked at John straight in the eyes and said, "John I am going." Finally, she managed to say her goodbyes and he left scowling at her with his coat collar up and his head held high. She watched him stalk off. That was the last she saw of John.

Matilda thought of becoming a governess. Marriage scared her. She had seen too many of her friends marry and divorce, and being a child of divorce, did not see marriage in her future. To her, marriage was a commitment and sacred.

Matilda had prepared herself to stay as a nanny for one year, and save enough money to return to school. Her parents' struggles haunted her. They had no higher education or a special skill.

Matilda was determined to educate herself. Her motto was to work hard at whatever she chose to do. Knowing she was not a brilliant child, did not faze her. Determination to succeed empowered her. As for her shyness, it was still a battle.

She became apprehensive when she thought of when she would leave the Evergreens. School began in September. She tried to rehearse what she would tell Richard. She knew how much she was needed, and it would be wrenching to leave. "I'll think about what I'll do when we return from Miami." These were her thoughts that nagged at her, which she often said out loud when alone.

"Is everyone ready?" Joey and Jennie were fighting over a toy. "Now listen both of you. If you keep this up, we shall miss the plane and you won't get to Grandma's hotel on the beach. I'm counting."

After Richard counted to three, the children ran to the front door. Matilda helped with the luggage, while Richard checked the house. Satisfied that all was in order, he closed the doors and locked up.

Fourteen

Arriving in Florida

"Wow," said Joey when the plane touched the ground.

"Hold on to Matilda while I get the luggage," yelled Richard. Matilda led the children, and Richard carried the suitcases.

"I'm going to be pilot when I grow up 'cause I want to fly through the clouds." Joey shouted out.

"Sounds wonderful," answered Matilda.

"Hey, look who's here." Janet and Ron Rosen held out their arms to their grandchildren. Joey stiffened up but Jennie reached out to her grandparents and was immediately smothered with kisses. Ron Rosen ruffled Joey's hair and put his arm about him.

"Oh, how you two have grown," said Janet kissing them. "Come on, let's get going." They stepped on the moving stairway that would take them to the airport exit.

Flying thrilled the children. They had come to Miami yearly, but were too young to be curious about their surroundings. People were dashing hurriedly in all directions, lugging their belongings.

"I'm hungry. I want a pretzel," whined Joey.

"Not now." Their father did not want them to eat snacks, but Joey continued to plead. Finally, Janet handed Joey two dollars.

"Okay. Here, buy two pretzels."

Richard frowned, but said nothing. He knew the children were going to be spoiled this whole week so he relented.

Outside the airport, Matilda glanced at the palm trees and felt the warmth of the sun on her face. "How lovely everything looks. What's the temperature?" she asked.

"Seventy degrees, said Ron. You like this eh?" questioned Ron

"I certainly do," replied Matilda.

The white Lincoln Continental was a comfortable ride to the hotel. Matilda felt like a child heading for her first carnival ride. She observed all the sights and wondered what the names of the luscious flowers were. Inside her purse was a camera and journal which she planned to use at every chance.

Jennie clasped her hand. Joey sat with his grandpa who was telling him about Florida and what they would soon see. Joey listened in awe at what his Grandpa said. Richard smiled.

"He looks better already," thought Matilda.

"Come on." Janet led them to the house enjoining the hotel. "I'll show you where your rooms are."

"I thought we were going to stay in the hotel," said Richard.

"Not this time. All the rooms are filled. Jacob and Aaron aren't coming home this holiday. They are off skiing in Colorado. There's plenty of room in the house."

"It's empty without my children. Mark is the only one who lives here." Janet turned to Matilda. "Sarah was raised here. Her room is just the same. I haven't touched a thing in it. I can't bring myself to remove anything yet. Joey and Jennie can see it when they have settled in."

Richard looked surprised but was pleased they were all going to stay in the house with a view of the sea. Janet gave him Jacob's room where he could watch the boats sail out.

He dropped off his luggage and opened the door to Sarah's room. He felt her presence. Filling the room was the scent she had liked to use. It was though she was next to him, and would appear and look up at him with her beautiful smile.

"Why was she taken from me?" He lay on her bed and cried while his head rested on one of the blue satin pillows; exhausted, he dozed off.

Awakened by a voice calling, he rubbed his eyes and stretched. It was his mother-in-law. Dazed, his eyes wandered over his dead wife's room where they fell on a collage of photos at different periods of Sarah's life. He felt distraught and empty as he stared at the pictures. Not having Sarah was beyond pain.

He remembered clearly the day of Sarah's illness. It was on a Tuesday, one of the hottest days in July. Sarah had a dreadful headache when he left. Richard thought it was the heat. Sarah never liked the hot summers. She took two aspirin and lay down with cold compresses. It was one in the afternoon when Sarah called him. She sounded very weak. He had rushed home to find his wife on their bed unable to move. The children were beside her. In a panic, he took them to a neighbor's house and hurried back to his wife.

"This pain is hell. I feel so weak. I can't seem to move."

Richard wasted no time. He carried her to the car and drove to the emergency room, running through red lights to get to the hospital. He had never seen Sarah so ill. She was admitted and lapsed into unconsciousness. Doctors had tried everything. Nothing worked, and by the evening Sarah was dead. A rabbi and minister came to comfort Richard who was in shock.

Sarah's parents flew in and made the funeral arrangements. His father-in-law was unable to talk, and his face remained void and drawn. It had been the hardest week in Richard's life. Richard's parents arrived later. They took over the care of his children. On his wife's bed in this sunny room, he relived it all.

The trauma of that week ran by him like an old movie. Richard felt an agonizing pain in his stomach. He got up and straightened his clothes, and went to the bathroom to freshen up. His eyelids were swollen and red, so he bathed them. He did not want anyone to see that he had been crying.

"Richard, are you coming down?" It was his mother-in-law calling. He hadn't unpacked. He sat down again and mumbled a silent prayer. He asked God to help him through his grief. After the sudden death of Sarah, he immersed himself in his new business. His parents had been his shield while he worked, and Richard had closed his mind that Sarah was gone. There was a light tap on the door. Janet entered.

"Hi. I wondered if you were all right. I thought you'd like a cold drink. How's the room?" Janet handed Richard the drink.

"The view is terrific. Thanks for giving me it."

"Oh, we want you to be comfortable, Rich."

"Where are the children?"

"The children and Matilda went down to the pool. They changed into their bathing suits faster than hares. You still haven't changed. Take a break. Go and enjoy the pool."

"Great, I will. It looks fabulous."

Fifteen

Ron and Janet Rosen

Grandpa Rosen was in the hotel pool with his grandchildren. Their squeals were heard clear to the house.

"What's going on, Ron?" asked Richard.

Richard sat down on a deck chair. It looked like the children were having fun. He called his father-in-law by his first name. He could not go along with the tradition of addressing his in-laws as mother or father.

"How's the hotel doing?"

"Great. Mark works very hard keeping all the accounts. He's a great help. The hotel is full, now. All our regulars are here for the season. My hope is that my other two sons join the business. I sure could use them. You know, Jennie is getting to look more and more like Sarah. I wish you would move here, Richard. You would be such an asset."

Richard smiled. "Who knows? Right now I'm getting my computer company off to a good start, and I like living where the seasons change. Twinsburg is a lovely city. I have lots poured into the business, and the bank would like the loans paid, so I must make it work."

"Maybe I can help you out. Just say the word."

Richard grinned at Ron. He felt grateful at the offer, but knew he had to make it on his own. This is what he wanted, and was willing to put the hours in.

"Thanks, I'm fine." Richard looked around at the sunbathers.

Children were gathered around the pool with their parents playing games with them. Jenny was sitting on her grandfather's shoulders, and Joey splashed water everywhere.

"That's enough of that, Joey. Don't be so rough. I'm going to change and when I come back, I'll give you a swimming lesson." Matilda sat at the edge of the pool and watched the children.

Florida was a welcome sight for Matilda. Her eyes soaked in the palm trees, the exotic water fountain with a statue of Eros, and the splendid house next to the Skylight Inn. "This has to be paradise," thought Matilda. It seemed that her lifestyle had changed in an instant, and she felt grateful to be in Miami.

Richard returned ready to swim. He approached Matilda. "Take a swim in the adult pool. I'll watch the children."

"Thanks, Richard."

Matilda floated on her back and looked up at the white clouds. As a child she would search them and see shapes of figures in them. She was too young to understand a scientific explanation on what was in a cloud. Clouds were a mystery to her.

An excellent swimmer, Matilda enjoyed the opportunity to return to a pool and exercise. Suddenly she heard a scream. Richard called out to her. She saw Richard bending over Jennie who was lying on the hard cement. Matilda put her hand over her mouth and felt her heart thumping as she ran.

She reached Jennie who was crying and clinging to her father. When she saw Matilda, she flung her arms to her. Matilda held her and carried her into the house. A large bump protruded from her forehead.

Janet Rosen heard her granddaughter cry.

"What happened?"

"Quick, get some ice," called Richard. "She fell on the wet walk, running after a ball." He carried her to the house.

He was relieved that Jennie was all right, but Matilda's hands were trembling.

"There, there, Jennie, grandma has you." Janet soothed her and rocked her gently.

Matilda excused herself and went to her room to change while Richard examined the injury.

"Should we take her to the doctor?"

"No, her forehead is swollen a little, but it will go down. Don't worry Richard, she's a little scared but that's all." Janet held a bag of ice firmly on the bump that was getting steadily larger.

"How is she?" asked Ron.

"She seems okay," replied Janet to her husband, who was puffing hard. "She has hurt her head and we are putting ice on it."

Ron's face became drawn. "Are you sure?"

"Of course I am. I've raised four children, and seen all kinds of falls that little ones get. Jennie will be fine."

"It looks like we have begun our vacation with a big bang," said Richard. He tried to be calm.

"We planned to show you around the hotel and then take a ride around Miami. Tomorrow should be good. I'm sure Jennie will be okay. How about it? Mark wants to see you and the children."

"I'm not sure about anything right now."

"Richard, trust me. Jennie will be fine." Janet opened the refrigerator and opened a box of popsicles, and gave one to Jennie. It was then Jennie's tears melted away.

Sixteen

The Two Holidays

"Who's going to light up the first candle?" Janet glanced at Joey. "Me." Joey raised his hand. "And Jennie can light the next one," commented Janet. Richard held Jennie's hand as she lit the Hanukkah candle while her grandparents read the prayer books.

"Here's your first present."

"We have seven more don't we, Grandpa?" asked Joey.

"You sure do. Happy Hanukkah everyone," said Ron.

It was a pleasant evening as the family sat down to the first night's celebration of Hanukkah, but Ron felt uneasy as he looked at the empty chair that should have been Sarah's. He ate little, but his eyes stayed glued on his grandchildren. Their chatter warmed his heart. Tomorrow morning, he would take them to see the Christmas tree.

"Come on, are you are all ready? Let's go to the hotel. I told Mark to expect us at nine o' clock sharp. It's decorated for Christmas."

"Come here. Let me see your forehead. That bump looks better, Jennie." Her grandmother gently touched her head.

"It looks likes she's grown an egg," yelled Joey, and gave his sister a punch with his fist.

"Stop that, Joey. If you touch your sister again you'll stay in your room, and grandpa won't take you anywhere." said Richard.

"I didn't do anything. She pushes me and you don't say anything to her. It's not fair. I don't want to see some beat up old tree."

Joey ran out of the house in the direction of the pool with his grandfather chasing after him. He reached a sandy section set aside for children. Joey began to cry. "Come here, boy." Ron took Joey by the shoulders.

"What's the matter?"

"Nothing is. Why can't every one leave me alone?"

"Look, we only have a few days together, and I have so much I want to show you. I need your company. Jennie is hurt and as you're her big brother, she needs you to be good to her. Do you understand, Joey?"

"Yep, I do."

"Now let's go in and you apologize." Ron Rosen knew exactly how Joey felt. He still ached for Sarah. "Come on, I'll take you to the hotel and you can see your Uncle Mark."

"Is Dad coming?"

"Why, of course."

"Are Jennie and Matilda coming?"

"Of course they are."

"Okay, I guess I'll go."

"That's my boy." Ron felt pleased that he had calmed his grandson.

Mark Rosen sat by the counter working on the computer where guests signed in. He called an employee to take over. A tall pine tree stood by the entrance, decorated with bright lights, silver ornaments, and a gold star. Above it was a large crystal ceiling lamp that shed beams of light. In the foyer, Christmas decorations glowed.

"Hi, what happened to Jennie?" Mark came forward to greet his sister's children.

"That's a big bump on her head. Don't you think she should see a doctor?"

"You know, I wanted to take her to a doctor, but your mother seems to think it's just a small bump and will go down."

"Come on, Richard. I'll call our family doctor and let him check it to be sure."

"Great, I'll feel better when she's examined."

Mark made the call, and an appointment was made for the afternoon. He turned to welcomed Matilda to the hotel. He was impressed, and thought what a lovely girl they have to care for the children.

Seventeen

Jennie's Ordeal

Doctor Powell examined Jennie. "There is a small cut."

He asked if she had thrown up, and if there had been bleeding from the wound. "Don't let her run around for a couple of days."

Dr. Powell gave Jennie a complete physical. "Call me in two days if she does throw up. She does not seem to have a head injury. Keep her in a sitting position or put a large pillow under her head when she sleeps."

"Thanks, Mark, for getting us to your doctor. I feel better about it. Jennie can rest up." Richard gave his daughter a comforting kiss. Matilda picked her up and held her close.

Janet knew that Jennie was all right, and it was unnecessary to visit the doctor, but said nothing more about it to Richard.

"She can stay with me on the lounge swing. Grandpa wants to take you all sight seeing, so go! Matilda you go, and see Miami. Go on, Matilda, have fun. Ron will take you."

"I think I'll stay put. I'm enjoying the porch and the view of the ocean. It's so relaxing. Tomorrow, I'll be ready to tour."

Richard read Jennie a story and made some phone calls to Twinsburg, and they ate lunch on the porch.

"This is what I really need. Now a boat ride out to sea would make everything perfect. It would take the edge off if I could drift out there. Yeah, that's what I'd like. How about it Grandma? Do you have any ideas?"

"Certainly, Ron can line up a boat. Some of our friends own yachts and ask us to go out. Usually, I refuse because we are too busy. Ron likes to fish when he has a chance, but as you know, he has done nothing much of late. Let me see what I can arrange."

"Matilda, what do you think of Miami?" asked Janet.

"It's just incredible." Matilda picked up Jennie. "How are you, sweets?"

Matilda sank into the lounge chair. She felt content to hold Jennie on her lap, and know that she would be fine. Matilda closed her eyes and listened to the waves drifting in. To her, the ocean was like a beating heart. Soon, she was sleeping, so Jennie got off her lap.

"Richard, I'm so glad you have Matilda caring for the children. She seems to be doing so well with them. It's wonderful that you found such a capable girl," remarked Janet. She removed her sun glasses and smiled.

"Well, that was my mother's doing. She's fussy; she selected her. We have gotten attached to Mattie. She has done lots for Joey. He's been a mess without his mother. I'm not doing too well either. She was my soul mate."

"Yes. I know. Sarah was a wonderful girl; she filled her life, and she would want you to enjoy yours, so you must make an effort Richard."

Janet felt much compassion for her lonely son-in-law, and wished she could come up with something positive.

"Tell you what, later today, I'll show Jennie and Joey pictures of their mother. They are in her room in her old chest. I think they will get a kick at seeing what she looked like when she was their age."

"That sounds fine, Janet."

Richard knew he could not enter the room again. Then he wondered if he had made the right choice in coming to Miami Beach. There were just too many memories here.

Ron joined the family. "Here are our tickets for the Everglades. Jennie is much better, so she can come, too."

Janet smiled at Ron, and swung open the porch door. "Come on upstairs children. I want to show you your mother's room."

Eighteen

Memories of Sarah

The children stood quietly looking over the tastefully decorated room. Mrs. Rosen found the albums in Sarah's chest, and presented them to the children. Joey asked numerous questions.

"Which photos do you want to keep?" Janet observed how hypnotized Joey was.

"All of them."

"Really, Joey, I don't think I can do that just yet."

"I will make a little album for you and Jennie to take with you, and the rest will be here when you come and visit. What do you think?"

That's cool," Joey replied.

"What's going on up there? I'm waiting to take you out to dinner. Hurry up," said Ron.

"We'll be right down. Well, Joey, how's everything so far?" Janet knew by just observing Joey's reactions that he was happy.

"I love it."

"Tomorrow, you are all off to the Everglades. I have things I must do, so I won't be joining you, but you can tell me all about it when you return."

The Everglades tired the children; they slept all the way back and awakened when the car stopped at the hotel. Ron was finally enjoying himself. Even though his feet ached, he was grinning. He saw the Everglades' beauty through his grandchildren's eyes.

Ron went into shock when Sarah died. The doctor sedated him, and he was unable to get out of bed. For two weeks he did not move.

Janet and Mark tried to get him up, but grief had swept him into depths of depression, and he refused to talk, eat, or leave his room.

Mark, his oldest son, took over the business of running the hotel, and proved capable at keeping it going. It was a long haul getting Ron to gain his strength and eat. He had been a tough, robust man who could handle anything. Sarah, his only daughter, was his life. Around her, he was a softie. Ever since her birth, he cared for her. Now she was dead.

Ron bathed and diapered his children long before it was vogue. He taught Sarah to ride her bike, tie her shoes, and how to fight her battles. Whenever he went on an outing, she came with her brothers. Furthermore, they knew she was his favorite. When the opportunity arose they would tease her unmercifully. Consequently, there was much friction between Sarah and her brothers while growing up. Only in adulthood did the tension leave among them.

Ron gradually showed improvement. Richard had the children telephone him. Their voices finally helped Ron out of his darkness. His grandchildren proved the best therapy.

Ron was stunned by Jennie's red hair and blue eyes. He picked her up and stood her on the sidewalk. "We're back. Let's see what Uncle Mark is up to."

"Well, it looks like that nasty bump is getting better." Mark was pleased to see the improvement, and so was Matilda.

"Come, let's get something to eat." Ron looked at Mark with pride, and was thankful he had a son unafraid to take on responsibility.

Since Sarah's death, Ron could not concentrate. He had lost thirty pounds, and his doctor kept a close watch over him. Slowly, he began to get his appetite back. Mark had been his lifeline. It was Mark who kept the hotel under control. Without him, Ron knew that it would have sunk into oblivion.

Hamburgers and fries were munched by the children in the hotel restaurant. Matilda ate a salad, and Ron ate a hearty bowl of chicken noodle soup. He was beginning to feel his old self.

"What are you two doing tomorrow?" asked Mark. Both children chimed in. "The beach!"

"Way to go. How I would like to go with you and your nanny." Matilda looked down because she felt her face redden. How she wished this would not happen.

"Are you ready for the ocean, Matilda?" asked Mark.

Matilda's expression said it all. "Why, of course I am."

Mark was impressed on how pretty she looked in her orange and yellow sundress, and had difficulty looking at anything else. They said goodbye to Mark, .and were ready to see their Grandmother.

"Did you have fun at the Everglades? Tell me what you saw and did," said Janet sitting with her grandchildren. She waited for their response.

"I don't know," replied Joey.

Janet laughed. "Name something."

"I saw a coot, and an otter, and an alligator, and lots of birds, and a snake."

"I wrote some of the animals' names for them, and selected a guide book to help us identify the animals. They had fun." Matilda showed Janet the book.

"That's super." Janet gave the children a hug. "I put the albums together while you visited the Everglades, and have something else belonging to Sarah which I shall give them when they leave. I know they will enjoy the pictures. I have written notes by each one."

"Oh, the children will be pleased." Matilda sat and looked at Sarah's photographs, and could see that she was a lovely girl.

Nineteen

A Day at the Beach

Sand buckets, and ocean waves occupied the children. A variety of shells covered the beach. Vacationers were out collecting them. Matilda built a royal sand castle, working hard on it. The children brought up buckets of sand from the ocean and helped. Matilda took photographs while they played.

"Tomorrow our sandcastle won't be here." Matilda looked sad.

"Why not?" asked Jennie.

"Because the tide will come in and wash it out to sea."

"Don't let it happen, Matilda," cried Jennie.

"I can't do anything about it, Jennie. It's part of nature. But I'll build you another."

They strolled to the pier and watched the pelicans fly over. Joey found some seashells to take back to Ohio. At the end of the pier, they stood by the fishermen and saw them prepare their nets.

"Come on. It's time to go back. I don't want the sun to burn you. Let's see what your grandparents and dad are doing. Help carry the towels and buckets."

Matilda knew that this had been one of the best days of her life. They stopped by an ice cream parlor and selected vanilla cones. The children were content. Most of all, they were happy to have Matilda with them. She took time to explain the answers to their questions and played games with them.

Richard was waiting. "How's the beach?" Both climbed on their father and gave him a hug.

"We love it," said Joey. Ron gave Joey a toss and lifted Jennie up to see if she could touch the ceiling.

Mark joined them for dinner at the house, and was glad for the small break. Christmas Eve dinner was on his mind, and he told his father he had to make sure the catering was right. His eyes rested on Matilda. She had a fresh look about her; so, he found it difficult to stop staring at her.

"Say, Matilda, how about joining me for the dinner and dance on Christmas Eve." She caught Mark's smiling blue eyes. There was silence. Everyone waited for her answer.

"Oh, no, thank you. Sorry, but I need to care for the children."

"We can manage them. The hotel will look magnificent. Go and see it. Mark is making this a lovely evening for our guests and has created a delicious menu." said Janet. She was proud of the Skylight Inn. Mark had looked over the decorations earlier in the day.

"Well, if it's all right with all of you, I will be delighted to go." Matilda felt awkward.

Matilda wrote furiously in her journal about the events that had occurred in Florida since arriving, and now she entered Mark's name, placing a smiley face by the entry. She looked forward to the dinner dance and him. She had to admit that he was very attractive, and those eyes of his just leaped out at her.

Matilda wore her one black dress and a white pearl necklace with earrings that matched. Mark was waiting and watched Matilda come down the stairs. This was his evening to relax from decision making, and he was looking forward to it. He had grown tired of the long hours of work .He desired his father to return to the hotel.

Mark looked across at his father playing a game with Jennie and Joey. Ron had a smile on his face which Mark hadn't seen since the death of his sister.

"Matilda, you are looking splendid. Christmas Eve is lovely at the hotel ball. Guests bring gifts and place them around the tree at the entrance to the ballroom. A security guard keeps his eye on them. Let's take a look." Mark took Matilda's hand.

Matilda felt elated. The hotel was alive with elegant women in evening dresses with their hair groomed and perfumed. Men wore evening suits and bow ties. They took care to escort their partners to the Christmas tree. Mark glanced at the packages decorated in bright holiday paper.

"Look Matilda, here's one for you."

"Are you sure?"

Mark pointed to a small, silver package with a bright red bow. "Here, it says Matilda Wiggins."

"Oh," said Matilda.

"Come on, let's go in and find our table." He seated her. He then approached the band leader. After a wave to him, he proceeded to the kitchen. Matilda glanced at the Christmas gift and wondered when she should open it. Tables were adorned with green cloths, and vases of assorted flowers. Guests brought their presents to the tables. Sounds of laughter and conversation permeated the large room. Matilda was impressed with the decorations and lights. Her body moved to the music and beat of the band, and how she wanted to dance. The band was playing the old tunes that Sue Evergreen liked.

Christmas was her favorite season, and here she was in this fabulous hotel in Florida. She remembered when Emily told her there was no Father Christmas. She was so disappointed, and had difficulty accepting his nonexistence that she had cried bitterly, remaining in her room for hours, ignoring her mother's plea to open her door.

Mark returned and checked the menu. All was in order. Now, he could enjoy the evening. He gazed at Matilda and saw her beauty and goodness. He, like the rest of the family was pleased that Richard had been successful at locating this fine English girl. He knew she would like to dance, but had to tell her he had two left feet.

"Come on teach me some steps. I'll give it a try."

Mark had not dated for months. He was just too busy. Many girls called him, but he was disinterested. Matilda was very beautiful, but he saw her as the children's nanny, and not a girl he could date. Even so, he was smitten, and tried his best not to allow his feelings show.

Mark told himself he was too old for her, but wished otherwise. He danced a little, and was totally entranced with Matilda's style, but knew he could not master the latest dances. He was no Fred Astaire.

After dinner, Matilda opened her present. The family had planned this surprise for her. Inside the little box, Matilda found a delicate watch with her initials on it and a greeting card from all the Rosen family. She thanked him and gazed at his thoughtful blue eyes and handsome grin. She saw Mark as charming, and was appreciative for the lovely evening, and told him so. In fact, she was captivated by him.

Early Christmas morning, the children dashed downstairs giggling. They had tried to stay awake to listen for Santa Claus, but had fallen into a deep sleep.

"We missed Santa. Did he come?" Jennie asked.

"Of course he did," replied Joey.

In the family room, by the couch, a variety of Christmas presents were piled up.

"You two must have been really good. Look what Santa has brought you." Janet Rosen was as excited as her grandchildren. They tore open the boxes and shrieked. After they played with their toys, Ron found his cap and put in pieces of paper with the names of sights they could visit. "Pick one," he said, grinning.

Twenty

Mark Rosen

Matilda drank her coffee. "Well go on Joey, choose a piece of paper." Matilda nudged him. Joey held out his paper to his grandfather. Ron read out loud, "The Miami Sea Aquarium." "Okay, finish eating and we'll go."

"What's on the others?" asked Joey

"Well, I'm saving those for your next visit."

Joey gulped his milk and ran upstairs with Matilda and Jennie. Janet came out of the downstairs bathroom looking quite regal.

"Did they make a choice?"

"Sure did," answered Ron. "It's the aquarium."

"Richard is going to stay home and lounge by the pool and catch up with reading the newspapers and maybe take a swim." said Ron who began whistling, and suddenly stopped.

"Matilda said she had a wonderful time Christmas Eve, and was pleased with the watch and the company of Mark, honey. Isn't that great?"

"That's good. Well, everyone, let's get going. We have to return early. This evening I am volunteering at the hospital so my friends can celebrate Christmas."

Janet kept her grief to herself. She and Sarah had been very close; she missed her, but never talked about it. Janet knew that she had to be tough, and carried herself with dignity in public.

Janet worked at the hotel and volunteered, never taking a quiet moment on her own, but knew if she did, she would fall into too much thinking and deep despair.

Richard felt the tension leave. Coming to stay with his in laws had given him some rest. He had thought earnestly at what his mother-in-law had said. Sarah was unselfish and kind, but she had a fiery temper.

He chuckled to himself remembering her way of dumping his clothes out on the back porch. It cured him of his messy habit. She would often say, "How do you expect the children to learn to be neat if you don't pick up your clothes?" These thoughts ran through his mind as he strolled over to the hotel to see Mark.

"Hi Mark, how was the dinner? Did you dance with Matilda?"

Mark laughed. "Yep, I danced once. I'm a rotten dancer. It's time I took some lessons. No kidding, I'm going to do it. Be with you in a minute, Rich." Mark closed up a bound book that held his attention.

Richard sat on the couch and glanced at the people who had arrived at the hotel. He listened to the foreign voices, and noticed many guests from Japan.

Mark joined Richard. "It's Christmas Day and people are still calling for reservations for New Year's Eve. It's all booked. Business is good, Rich."

"I had the best time last night. Matilda is a doll. It's too bad that you are leaving. I wouldn't mind getting to know her. Her English accent is so nice."

"Well, that will be hard, Mark. We live too far away. What you need is a break from the hotel and an evening out with a pretty girl. I think your father will return to work now that he has seen his grandchildren. He seems to come to life around them."

"Running a family business and getting enough help is the hardest part. I was hoping that Jacob and Aaron would take a break from school and help out. It's getting monotonous," commented Mark "I was ticked off when they did not come, but I knew they needed to rest up and have a change. I remember what hitting the books was like. Still, they're playboys and a little selfish if you ask me. Hope they keep their promise and work after their graduation."

Mark returned to the desk and computer and studied the reservations. He seemed satisfied. "Come on, let's get some breakfast."

"What are you up to today?" Mark asked.

"It's the beach, man. It's the beach. Hope it's warm enough to swim," said Richard.

"Wish I could join you. One of these days I'll do just that." Mark straightened his tie and buttoned his suit jacket. Richard drank his black coffee and finished up the blueberry pancakes and got up to go.

Mark glanced at Richard and could see through his actions that he was grieving. Richard's eyes had deep circles from lack of sleep. Mark felt uncomfortable that he shared his emotions when his only sister had died. Still the stress he was under was taking its hold.

"See you later. Have a good one. It's back to work; this place is moving, man."

Richard stuck his cap on and loaded his camera.

"Think I'll take some pictures of the sights and take a load of the family tonight. See you later."

"Sure will," said Mark, walking back to his job.

Richard waded through the waves and shot some film. Crowds stretched over the beach, so he returned to the hotel pool. He dozed on the deck chair and was awakened by a sprinkle of rain on his face. He folded up the chair and moved to the outside porch to await the family. Solitude and the rain cleared his mind.

"We brought you some dinner. We knew you'd be hungry." Matilda thought Richard looked relaxed. The children cuddled up to their father while he tried to eat. Matilda held a bunch of postcards of Miami.

"If you don't mind, I'd like to write out these cards."

"Go ahead, take your time. Everything's under control." said Richard staring at the downpour.

Janet changed quickly to volunteer. "Come here Joey. Tell me what you will remember most about Florida." Joey thought for a second.

"Everything!"

"That's a lot. I'll be home later. Perhaps the rain will stop soon and you can take a walk with your grandfather?" Joey nodded.

"This week has gone too fast," announced Janet.

"Well, is everyone ready? The plane leaves for Cleveland in three hours." Richard dashed about searching for miscellaneous items and looked pleadingly at Matilda who searched her list.

"You do have a load, must be all those presents." Janet's eyes gleamed. She gave Joey his mother's class ring on a chain and a silver bracelet for Jennie. Albums of their mother were tucked in their suitcases.

"Have a great trip, and expect me to come to a football game." Mark gave a quick glimpse at Matilda. "And you, Matilda, can take me to the Rock 'n' Roll Hall of Fame. Come here you two and give your Uncle Mark a kiss." Mark knew that he had to see Matilda again, and soon. She had crept into his heart.

The plane soared into the clouds.

"I hate goodbyes. I hope we see them soon." On the way home, Janet talked nonstop.

Ron did not seem to hear anything his wife said. Traffic was heavy. Ron hit the radio button and caught the sport's results while Janet chatted on about their grandchildren.

When they returned to the house, Ron said nothing. He climbed slowly up the stairs to the bedroom and closed the door. It was as though the lights had gone out. Nothing was real. The jet had taken his joy away. Janet clutched at a chair and looked at the steep stairs. She, too, was overcome with the loneliness she saw in her husband.

The house was so quiet. She stood silently, and then sank into her deep wine leather armchair, and remained in it till dark. She finally arose and switched on the light and climbed the stairs. Ron had not left the bedroom.

Twenty-One

Returning to Winter

Matilda shut off the alarm. She thought about Miami Beach and sunshine. She pulled the blind and blinked, rubbing her eyes in disbelief at the snow that was whirling everywhere. It seemed too much reality to face. Richard had gone to a neighborhood New Year's Eve party and had slept most of the day.

She knew he would still be tired. She slipped on her robe and went to the bathroom and splashed her face with cold water and brushed her teeth. Their vacation was over. Tomorrow it was back to school for Joey.

Joey tumbled out of bed half asleep. He dressed, ate his breakfast, and went to see his father.

"Dad, I'm leaving."

"Okay, have a good day Joey. I will be a little late tonight because this is the first day back to work. Give me a hug."

"Bye, Dad."

Matilda could not remember Joey smiling when he went to school. It was a good feeling to see this change in him. Richard was up and showering while Jennie watched cartoons and held her bear. Matilda prepared breakfast. Richard came down and drank some coffee and left. He arranged to pick up the mail first and mentioned that his parents had sent the children their Christmas presents.

Richard was not pleased at all the gifts, and told Matilda when he brought them home to hide them away for a future date. He knew his in-laws would spoil the children so he decided to put a stop to the growing number of toys.

"What we'll do is have them select what they no longer play with and donate them. See what you can do, Matilda." She thought this was a splendid idea and said she would work on it.

At the end of the week, the playroom was clean. The children helped put their used toys in a large box and took them to the Salvation Army. Joey was proud that he had given away his old toys. Jennie had made a fuss, but finally relinquished some of hers. Richard congratulated them on cleaning the playroom.

Matilda's thoughts were on Florida and Mark. She wondered if he really meant to come to Ohio, or was he just being sociable. She had not heard a word from him and wondered if he would phone or visit soon. She tried to put him out of her mind, but all she could see were those blue eyes smiling at her.

Matilda had been back for a week. The dark foreboding skies depressed her. Discovering January in Ohio was difficult for her to adjust to. She looked out the windows and wished she could return to Miami Beach and Mark. The snow's arrival in November had excited her, but now she had enough.

Matilda grabbed the phone after it rang several times.

"How's everything going, dear? Did Richard pick up the Christmas gifts for the children? How did they enjoy them, and how was Florida? And you dear, did you have fun? Oh, how I miss my grandchildren. How are they getting along?"

Matilda tried to answer, but Sue did not stop for breath.

Sue told Matilda that she and Al would fly in to visit soon, but would rather wait until the weather improved in Ohio.

"How can anyone live in Cleveland in the winter? I just don't know how they do it. It's plain awful. I'm surprised that Richard would want to stay there. Now, dear, tell me what you all did in Florida. I want to know everything. No secrets!"

Matilda thanked her for the presents and told her she enjoyed Florida.

"Now tell me the truth. How is Richard? Is he brooding? Is he working too hard?" Sue queried.

Matilda hesitated. As far as I can tell, he seems to be just fine."

"Oh, that's good news Matilda. Thank you. Make sure he calls me this evening."

"Yes, I will."

"Bye, my dear."

MATILDA

Matilda stuck a note on the bulletin board. Sue doted on her only son. She had wanted more children, but it never happened.

Twenty-Two

Sue Evergreen's Ideals

Sue hung up the phone and sat down to drink her tea. She looked over yesterday's morning paper and studied the ads. She put the paper down. Perhaps she should sell her shop and move closer to Richard, but she knew she would not like living in a cold climate.

Besides, living in Hollywood, California was ideal for her. Sue had been star struck all her life, and had tried to become an actress. She appeared in small roles in the community theater, but the career she craved had gone no further. She met Al while singing in the musical, *Guys and Dolls*. After knowing each other for two months, they eloped causing much commotion on both sides of the families.

Al and Sue often flew to New York City on package tours to see the latest Broadway shows, but they had no intention of leaving Hollywood. When Sue was young, she was often told that she was the image of Doris Day.

Sue was never far from a mirror. Makeup and Sue were twins. She never left the house without it. Plastic surgeons were her savior. She had small surgeries over the years, and compliments were often bestowed upon her looks.

Recently, she'd had a face lift. Her appearance was most important, especially for the business. Society said "stay young," so she kept up her appearance and visited the gym three times a week, no matter how busy the shop became.

Sue examined the fashions, but knew she could not wear what was depicted in the magazines, so she dressed in colorful clingy dresses with chunky jewelry and large loop earrings. She would rather be dead than wear clothes designed for women over fifty.

Richard was her very life. She and Al saw to it that he had a good education. Al taught Richard the florist business and he helped out after school. When he earned his driver's license, he enjoyed delivering the flowers, but wasn't particularly interested in the business. More than anything, computers held Richard's attention.

The strain and distance of not being near Richard upset Sue. Al often tried to comfort her, but she missed her grandchildren. Even so, she knew that she had to fly to Twinsburg, soon. When Al came home from the barber's, she decided to make him listen to her concerns, but if there was a golf game, she would encounter a hard time catching his attention.

Sue poured herself another cup of tea, put her feet up on the kitchen chair, and turned to the entertainment section of the newspaper and read. It was ten before she began her chores. She had thought of hiring a cleaning company, but knew they would not satisfy her. She grumbled and moaned as she set out to get her housework done.

Twenty-Three

Ron Rosen

Mark threw down his pen. He could not do another thing. It was two a.m. He kicked off his shoes and collapsed on the office couch and slept. He awoke to a knock on the door, and a crack of light coming though the drapes.

"Just a minute," He called.

"It's me." It was his father's voice.

"Dad, what are you doing, here?"

"What am I'm doing? I have come to work."

"What are you saying, dad?"

"You heard me, boy, and it looks like you could do with a shower and a day off. Get going, now."

Mark looked at his desk calendar. It was February, and his dad had returned.

"Okay, Dad, I'm out of here."

Mark had waited patiently for this day. He went to the house, took a shower, dressed and walked along the beach and saw the sea gulls scream above him. The sea breeze brushed his shirt. It felt sensational. He could not believe that his dad was ready to come back. He took a deep breath and inhaled the salty air. "Yes. Yes. Yes. I'm free; hear that seagulls?"

Janet welcomed Mark with fresh coffee. He ate a full breakfast of orange juice, scrambled eggs and toast.

"What do you know, Mom, Dad's working."

"Yes, Mark, and I'm glad. I think he is going to be okay."

Mark sighed.

"It's wonderful Mom, but I guess he will have to break in slowly. At least today is a vacation for me. He told me to take off."

Janet laughed. "I'm going over there soon; the day is yours, Mark. Have fun."

Ron checked the mail in the office and talked with his secretary. It had been four months since Sarah had died. Gradually, he had wooed himself off the sedatives. He took out a cigar and sat back, smoked it, and then looked through some papers that Mark had clipped together.

Mark badly needed to replenish his wardrobe. He didn't mind shopping for clothes, so he decided to browse the mall. Matilda was on his mind; he wondered when he could take off to see her. In just a few short months, his brothers would be through school and then he could take a trip to Twinsburg. They called and said they would graduate in May. Both thanked him for working at the hotel.

Mark returned with packages containing a new pair of shoes, tee shirts, and some socks. He could not understand what happened to his socks. "What was with the washing machine? It must have a mouth," he thought. Odd socks were all he could locate in his cluttered up drawer.

He whistled as he entered the house. No one was home. He made himself a sandwich and settled on the sofa and watched some television. He wondered how his dad was getting along.

Ron finished going through the pile of papers, and felt pleased at what he saw. He knew what an asset Mark had been. The business had grown. Even though the season was over, there were banquets signed up for the next few months, and tours were coming in. Painters, carpenters and decorators worked all over the place, remodeling. Mark had kept it all going. His phone rang. He had ignored his messages so he could catch up. This time he answered it.

"Hi Dad, how are you feeling? Thought I'd just call to make sure everything was all right." said Mark.

"Boy, it's more that all right. "You have done a fantastic job. Come on over and let's talk."

Mark hung up and yelled "G-r-e-a-t!" He knew everything was going to be fine. He put on a pair of tennis shoes and rushed out the door.

Janet ran the hot water and soaked in the tub. It had been a long day. She closed her eyes and let the bubbles settle around her. She liked the public radio station and often listened to it a lounging in the tub. She preferred speakers that discussed politics. Often she thought of running for an elected office, but the hotel came first. She admired President Clinton, and thought he was doing a fine job for the country. The stock market was booming and she thought it time to buy some more stocks, but every time she read the newspaper, she'd find something negative about President Clinton. She put it down to politics. Dirty politics bothered her, so most of the time she voted as an independent.

Women who had become senators and house representatives impressed her. At Florida State, she majored in political science and wanted to study law, but when she began her family, she could not see continuing with her education. Women's liberation was a good thing, but she knew she could not do it all, so she chose motherhood.

She felt refreshed as she covered herself with a large bath towel.

"Janet, I'm home."

Janet put her thoughts aside as she called down to her husband of thirty eight years of marriage.

"I'll be down in a minute." She slipped on her comfortable blue terry cloth robe. She had not seen her husband in the hotel. Working on the computer in another office had kept her occupied, and she didn't want to disturb him on his first day back; nevertheless, she felt anxious.

One look at her husband told her that everything was going to be all right.

"How was it, dear?"

Ron pulled his wife close to him. Janet rested her head on his shoulder and began to sob. Her body shook as the pent up tears fell. She sobbed until there were no tears left. She fell upon the sofa exhausted. Her husband sat beside her. He gently held her close and stroked her head.

Janet had not shed a tear over her daughter's death, and had witnessed her husband fall into depression. Now, he was back to work. She believed that they could renew their lives and that the healing over their daughter's death might come. All along, she had tried to be brave.

Twenty-Four

Matilda's Plans

Matilda was thankful the repairman had gotten the part for the washing machine. She was finally able to get the laundry finished. Placing the bill on Richard's desk, she went upstairs to check on Jennie who was taking a nap.

Matilda sat by Jennie and reread Carrie's letter. Carrie wanted to know her plans. She had asked Matilda when she might take a holiday and come and see her and the family. Everyone was asking how she liked being a nanny.

Carrie had stopped by to see Matilda's mother and said she seemed fine, but was missing her daughter. Matilda held onto the letter. She thought about her finances. Right now, she could see no way of taking a flight home. She had enough money for the fare, but it was mostly for her education.

It looked as though it would be another year before she could even think of making the trip. She missed her family, friends, and London. She decided to write to her mother and Carrie after the children had gone to bed.

The door opened and Joey came in. Matilda had not realized the time. "My, it's good to see you Joey." He had some papers to show Matilda.

"Why, Joey, these are so good."

Joey had drawn figures of his grandparents in Florida with the ocean swirling about them.

"Shall we send these to Grandma?"

"Sure," answered Joey.

"Okay. Let's do it now."

Jennie was still sleeping, so Matilda found a large envelope and addressed it.

"It's all set, Joey. I'll mail it tomorrow." Joey beamed.

Strong winds forced Matilda to take Jennie home after only a short walk one March day. Matilda went to the bulletin board to check the calendar for appointments. September would be here in just a few months. She scanned through the calendar and knew she had to make inquiries about returning to school.

Matilda's impending plans were growing weaker each day. She worried constantly at what would happen when she left the children. Matilda knew she had to tell Richard and stop procrastinating, so he could find a replacement.

Richard came home early.

"How's everything today, Matilda? I thought I would take Joey to the park and play ball." On Fridays, Richard often closed the business early.

"By the way, Mark called and said he plans to come in for a long weekend. Apparently, Ron, my father-in-law, is running the hotel, so Mark is taking a mini vacation."

Matilda became quite flustered when Richard spoke of Mark. She stood there with her mouth wide open. She did her best to gain self control as she listened to what Richard had to say. Often she thought of Mark and his wonderful grin, but there had been no contact, and she wondered if she would ever see him again.

"He's flying in next weekend. We'll have to get the guest room ready. He mentioned that he'd like to see the Flats and the Rock-n-Roll Hall of Fame."

"It's good you have this big house. It gives you plenty of room for company," remarked Matilda. She was so excited that she accidently dropped a dish on the floor. It did not break. Richard picked it up.

"You are right. It's a great house. I'll just get a snack and take Joey and Jennie out." Jennie heard her father, and came down the stairs rubbing her eyes.

Matilda sat at the kitchen table drinking coffee. All she could do was think about Mark. She couldn't wait to see him. She remembered Mark's kindness, and admired his leadership qualities in the running of the Skylight Inn. He was mature, clever and handsome, and her stomach tightened just thinking of him, but she knew he was not for her.

She went to her room and looked through her clothes. Most of her attire consisted of jeans and shirts, for there had been no occasion to get dressed up. She looked at the pink dress and knew that was for a special event. Matilda desired to look pretty for Mark, but except for the one black dress that she wore at Christmas, she had nothing that she liked.

Matilda made a decision to take some cash out of her small account and buy some new clothes. Matilda realized that Saturday was a good day to shop. It was her usual day off, so she looked forward to having fun.

Twenty-Five

Mark's Visit

Mark's plane arrived on time.

"Did you bring some sweaters with you, Mark? The weather has been a little crazy. The winds have been whipping about the house. I thought that I would lose some shingles."

"I have all I need. How's everything going? How are the children?"

"They are doing much better, thanks to the visit to their grandparents. They seem okay. How are you?" Mark patted Richard on the back.

"I'm fine. I'm looking forward to visiting some Cleveland highlights. Richard, if you can spare Matilda for a couple of days, I'd like to take her around."

"Why, you devil. She has the weekends off, and Linda comes over. It will be entirely up to her. She is usually home in the evenings, but I think we can spare her." Richard grinned. "I thought you wanted to come here for a game. Hey man, you seem to have other interests! The stadium is always packed on weekends. The Browns are not doing too well. Still, the fans love 'em," said Richard.

"Well, maybe I can catch a game on my next visit."

"Look who has come to see us. It's your Uncle Mark," said Richard. Matilda welcomed him and shook his hand.

The children greeted him. Matilda's eyes lit up and her gestures could not be hidden. Mark noticed the special look she gave him.

She wore a dark green sweater and tailored slacks and her silky black hair was pulled up entwined in a green bow.

"Are you getting ready for St Patrick's day?" Mark was enamored with her appearance.

"No, I like wearing green, but I do have some Irish heritage. My great grandparents were from Ireland, and yes, I plan to celebrate Saint Patrick's Day, too."

"It is very becoming on you. You should wear green often." Mark looked at Richard and said, "Don't you agree?"

Matilda had the table set in the dining room, with Sabbath candles lighted. She remembered how the Rosen family celebrated Sabbath on Friday night, and how generous Mark's family was. She wore the watch given to her by the Rosens, and told Mark that it kept perfect time.

"Wow, this is very nice, and the chicken soup and noodles are great," said Mark.

Matilda had found a recipe in a cookbook and carefully followed every detail for soup and roast chicken. She baked an apple pie, and felt pleased the crust turned out right.

Richard and Mark cleared the dinner table and washed the dishes.

"You deserve a break after this sensational dinner," said Richard, seeming pleased.

"Thanks, I'll take the children upstairs and read to them. They so enjoy Dr. Seuss."

"Everything has been put away. Matilda, how about a walk around the block? You can tell me where you are taking me tomorrow?"

Matilda looked at Joey and Jennie.

"They need to get ready for bed, Mark."

"I'll do that, Matilda." Richard crossed the room and pulled Joey over to him. "How's my boy doing?" Joey rolled on the floor with Richard and they began to wrestle. Jennie squealed as she watched them play.

"Come on, Matilda. Get your coat."

The houses on the street had gas lamp lights which gave the houses a golden glow against the cold night. The wind had stopped howling.

"Are you warm enough?" Mark pulled Matilda's hood closer to her head.

"I'm getting used to the cold. Spring will be here soon. The trees are already full of buds. I saw a robin today which was just wonderful! The snow has finally gone. I was not aware how bitterly cold, Ohio winters are. No wonder people take off to Florida."

"Yes, and I'm glad they do. It's good for our hotel. We get many who travel from the Cleveland area. They call them Snow Birds. Tell me, Matilda, what are your plans? Will you be staying here say for another year?"

Matilda was surprised at this question.

"Well, I have been thinking about lots of things, but I haven't made a decision, yet. The children are doing so well, now, that it will be hard for me leave. In September, I probably will register for classes to become a governess. I would like to teach. Somewhere in the future, I might decide on becoming an elementary school teacher. There are many universities here to select from."

"There you are, a girl with some fine plans."

Mark was mesmerized by Matilda's beauty. He loved her. There could be no one else for him. Tomorrow, he would find just the right time and place and propose marriage. There was no way he would let her go. He was becoming impatient to claim the woman he loved.

Mark had purchased a one-carat diamond ring, which he had tucked in a pocket of his suitcase. He had not concerned himself with the size because he knew the ring could be adjusted to fit Matilda's petite finger. At thirty-four, he felt like a teenager.

Marriage had been the last thing he'd wanted, but in Matilda, he'd found his love and hoped she would consent to marry him. She might leave for England, or go somewhere with no forwarding address. No, he could not let her go.

"What's it like? Is it getting colder? Mark, you must feel cold after Florida's sun. Can I mix you a drink?" Richard asked.

"No thanks, but I wouldn't mind something warm. Hot chocolate would be good."

Mark didn't sleep much. He punched his pillow to get comfortable, but all he could think of was choosing the right words when he proposed marriage to Matilda. All night he stared at the ceiling. If Matilda agreed to become his wife, how could she leave the children? Richard had repeatedly mentioned how much Matilda had worked with Joey, and the change had finally come. Joey was secure because of her.

Mark could not taste his breakfast and was in a black mood. He spilled coffee on his new shirt. Here his love sat across from him, but there was no joy. Tucked in his pocket was the diamond ring.

"Want to read the sports section, Mark?"

"Sure."

Richard handed him *The Plain Dealer* newspaper.

"It looks like a clear day for sightseeing. You and Matilda have fun. Oops, there goes the doorbell. It must be Linda. I'll get it. I have to go. See you all later."

Mark and Matilda took off in Matilda's Toyota. Matilda directed with a map of the Cleveland area. She felt happy to be sitting next to Mark.

She thought about her future and dared not imagine Mark in it. He lived an entirely different life from hers. He was mature with accomplishments behind him. She had yet to meet her goals. Nevertheless, Mark's handsome profile held her attention. His nose was small and he had a dent in his chin. When he smiled, he lit up the room for her. His voice was direct and clear. "Oh, he's too perfect! No, he's not interested in me. He's a man of the world. He just wants to see what it is like to date an English girl." Matilda became apprehensive.

Mark found a parking spot. "Come on, Matilda, let's tour Cleveland."

"Have you come downtown before?"

Matilda was glad she was wearing comfortable shoes. "Yes, to a football game, but nowhere else."

"So where do you want to go first?"

"Let's see the Rock and Roll Hall of Fame," replied Matilda.

Both enjoyed the museum of music. They walked to the harbor. Mark took Matilda's hand in his.

"You know something, Matilda, You are such a beautiful girl that you should not go out alone."

"I bet you have told that to many girls," replied Matilda.

"No, not since I was sixteen," answered Mark.

They approached the harbor. "Cleveland is a lively city. There are lots to do here. Suppose you take me to the art museum tomorrow, or maybe we could catch a matinee at one of the theaters."

Mark searched Matilda's eyes. "It's your choice, Matilda."

"The theater would be great."

"All right, I'll see what I can line up. Are you hungry? Let's go to the Flats and select a restaurant."

The Bluebell overlooked the river.

"How do you like this place?" asked Mark. They had the waiter select a table by a window.

"It's grand."

"Matilda, look at me. I don't know how to say this, but I, have missed you since you returned to Twinsburg. And oh, what am I saying? Matilda, when I saw you with the children, and how you deeply cared for them, I thought that girl would make a wonderful mother, and when you came to the dance on Christmas Eve looking so ravishing, I was just hooked. Matilda, I love you and want you to marry me."

Matilda gasped. Mark took her hands and kissed them.

"Matilda, say you will marry me."

"Mark, I'm confused. I don't know what to say. Why, you don't know me, or I you. And marriage is not in my plans right now," whispered Matilda.

"Matilda I think your plans can be altered. I fell in love with you the fist time I saw you, and I believe you are a little in love with me. I understand you know nothing about me, but you will have a lifetime to cure my bad habits."

"Yes, but the children."

"What about them? They will be in your life always. Richard will find another nanny. You will see that everything will work out."

"Just let me hear you say you love me, Matilda. At least say something."

Mark looked into Matilda's enormous brown eyes and waited. There was silence.

"Mark, I do love you, but I hadn't thought of marrying for a long time."

"Matilda, how long is that?"

"Not until my education is over."

"My darling Matilda, come to Miami. You can receive all the education you need. I won't stand in your way. In fact, I shall demand you study every day. Only please say you will marry me."

Mark felt in his jacket pocket for the ring. "Here, my sweet. I took the liberty of selecting an engagement ring."

Matilda hesitated for a moment. "Oh, Mark, I do love you but..."

"Then, you will marry me, Matilda?"

Mark placed the ring on Matilda's finger and kissed it. "It fits. The prince chose the right size." Matilda gazed at the ring's glitter as the sun's bright ray shone through the window.

"Mark, the ring is just beautiful. I will treasure it. Right now, I'm speechless." Matilda had not sad yes. The ring said it for her.

"Well, let me hear you say you will marry me."

"Oh yes, Mark! I will!"

Twenty-Six

Mark's News

Richard drove Mark to the Cleveland Airport early Monday morning. He didn't say much. Mark's announcement that he and Matilda were engaged stunned him. Eventually, Matilda would leave, he knew that, but not to marry Mark. Richard wondered if Mark was in his right mind, having only known Matilda for a week.

Sue Evergreen answered the phone. She was sleepy and wondered who would call so late. She had just put on her lounge pajamas, and was watching the television evening news. "Why, Richard, how good it is to hear your voice." Immediately, Richard spoke of Mark's engagement to Matilda.

"Wow! That's surprising news. Congratulations. Matilda is a special girl. She will make a good wife for Mark, and to think that I played cupid."

"Mother, what are you talking about? This whole thing is ridiculous. I hope Mark comes to his senses. He is at least twelve years older then she, and what does Matilda know about living here. Besides, I can't give up Matilda. She is everything to the children. Joey's behavior is much better. Matilda has been the calming influence on him. She is a marvelous nanny."

"Richard, don't worry, we are planning to come in soon, and we'll stay longer than usual and I will find you another nanny. I doubt if Matilda will get married right away. She is not the kind of girl to leave you without getting a good nanny."

"If Matilda had not gone to Florida, none of this would have happened."

"Richard dear, love is not planned. It happens."

"Mom, you are making me mad."

The receiver slammed in Sue's ear.

Mark Rosen met his father at the hotel foyer. The Skylight Inn was bustling. It attracted plenty of visitors. On the walls were photos of singers who had sung in popular bands, and had toured the country. Autographs were scrawled over glamorous pictures, which smiled at visitors when they entered. Guests were curious about them and pointed to certain photographs and asked when the artists appeared at the hotel. It was an eye pleaser.

"Well, how was your weekend, Mark? Did you like the weather there? Tell me how my grandchildren are. I bet they have grown again. Think your mom and I will go see them soon."

Mark smiled at his dad. "Dad, got a minute to sit down?"

"Sure. Let's get some coffee. Mark, everything is just rolling. I'm almost back to where I was. Now when Aaron and Jacob come, it will be even better."

They drank their coffee. "Well, you can tell me about your weekend. Come on. I'm waiting for all the details." Ron smiled at his son.

"Dad, are you ready for a great surprise?"

"Sure, tell me."

"Dad, I am engaged to Matilda Wiggins."

"Richard's nanny?" What? I can't believe it. When did this happen?"

"Saturday evening. All I can say, it was love at first sight."

Ron let out a burst of laughter. "Mark, you had me convinced that you would remain a bachelor. Did that little lady convince you to change your mind?"

"No, not exactly, I convinced her to marry me. She's too precious and gorgeous for me to let her get away."

"Oh, I see. The best thing that man created is marriage. It's better all around. Still, are you sure that she is the one? After all, Mark, you have only known her week. Aren't you rushing things?"

"Dad, with Matilda, I feel as though I've always known her. I just can't explain it, but I know I love her."

"Have you thought about her family in England and what they will say?"

"No, but it will be interesting to meet them."

"I think that you need to get to know her before you rush into marriage. What's got into you to do such a hasty thing?"

"Dad, it's love."

"Well, it looks like you have made up your mind."

"Yes, I have. Now I'll go and tell Mom."

Janet put on her makeup and tried to get enough light to work on the mascara to touch up her eye lashes. She wore her brown hair up in a bun. Her pretty ears showed off her aqua earrings. At fifty-eight, she was quite lovely. She picked up her purse to go to the hotel. As she looked out the window, she saw Mark. She was always happy to see her beloved eldest son.

Mark opened the door and gave his mother a broad smile. Within seconds of entering, he told her of his engagement to Matilda.

"Why, Mark, are you crazy? Are you joking? Matilda is just a nanny. That's all. Why she is probably here on a green card, and will return to England. You are making a terrible mistake. There are wonderful talented girls right here. You have dated many. You just have not found the right one, but you will. And what's more, you know nothing of her background. Mark, Mark."

Mark had turned his back on his mother. Janet just stared after him. She felt he would surely think it over and know that she was right. Mark had always listened to her, and would come to his senses. It was just a fling and a bad one. She would make sure nothing would come of it.

As for her son, she was aware he had spent too much time in the hotel. That was his problem. He knew many girls from good families, and no doubt would marry one. This she was sure of. She felt confident he would never marry Matilda Wiggins. In fact, she would do everything in her power to make sure there would be no marriage. She checked herself in the mirror. Satisfied with her appearance and decision, she left for the hotel.

Twenty-Seven

Spring in Ohio

Mrs. Miller came on time.

"Hi, Matilda, ain't it a nice day? Did you get me some cleanin' stuff? You need to tell me when you want me to help with the spring cleanin'. Ain't it nice to see them buds on the trees? Everthin' is just popping out all over the place. Twinsburg's such a lovely place, ain't it? Richard's parents will see a sparklin' house when they get here. I got the Midas touch."

"If you can come again on Friday, it would be perfect. They're arriving here Saturday. "Is Friday okay?" asked Matilda.

"No problem, I'll finish up. Just give the kitchen some shine and I'll be done," said Mrs. Miller.

"I knew this was the best time to come." Sue Evergreen checked her hair in the mirror. She wore her purple dress which looked perfect. Her perfume was thick, and as she walked through the airport the scent curled in the air. They sat down and waited for the rented car. Sue nudged Al to straighten up his shirt collar.

Al never took his eyes off the paper as he read the sports section and saw what the professional golfers were up to. He fixed his collar, and returned to reading. Al knew what Sue would say before she spoke. He had a habit of saying "Yes Sue, you're right."

"I just can't wait to see Richard and the children," said Sue.

Al folded up the *Plain Dealer* newspaper. The car was ready. They rented a red Chevy Monte Carlo. He opened the trunk and put the luggage in.

"It's great to be on the ground. Just look at those daffodils, Al, take a deep breath."

Al smiled at his wife. He loved her as much as ever. She was always reminding him of the little things, and it was a good that she did. He knew he would be lost without her. He drove up the driveway. The house looked impressive. Everything had a sparkle to it.

"How lovely the house is, Matilda, and the children look just grand. This must be all your doing. I knew I was right to have selected you, Matilda, dear. After lunch, I will take a nap, and when I'm rested, you can tell me all about you and Mark and when you are to be married."

Matilda had written to Carrie and her mother of her engagement and sent pictures of Mark. They wrote back stating they were both shocked and surprised, but offered their congratulations. Carrie had underlined in her letter. "I thought you did not want to get married for a long time."

Of course they were right, but she had fallen hopelessly in love with Mark, and marrying him was the right thing for her. She missed him and could not wait for the weekend when he planned to come up.

Mrs. Evergreen came downstairs looking rested. "I'm not like I used to be. Traveling and packing simply drains me, and this time I brought two large cases as I don't know how long we are going to stay. We have a wonderful manager now, who I completely trust. Isn't that wonderful, Richard?"

"Yes Mom, it is. Thanks for coming in. The children are always glad to see you." Richard had accepted the fact that Matilda would be off to Miami and would marry Mark. He knew that Mark and Matilda were both good people, and having Matilda join the family would be fine.

Richard questioned if it would be necessary to look for another nanny. He thought he might be able to manage on his own after September, but knew his mother would come up with some good ideas on how to handle it.

"Joey, have you played any golf?"

"No grandpa. I play football with Dad."

"Well in that case, Joey, you go find your clubs. We are going out tomorrow and play a game."

Joey was pleased. Jennie climbed on her grandmother and asked her to read her bear book. Sue looked warmly at Matilda, admiring her beauty. "Matilda dear, let me see your ring."

"Oh, I don't wear it around the house for fear of the diamond getting chipped. I have it upstairs in my jewelry box. I'll show it to you. Next weekend Mark will be coming in."

"Is that so?" Where is he going to stay?"

"He is going to sleep on the hide-a-bed in the family room. He said he wants to see you. It's almost a month since I have seen him. We would like to get our wedding plans organized."

"Oh, I see. Have you selected a place for the wedding?"

"Mark would like us to marry at the Skylight Inn in the ballroom at Christmas. It is beautiful. Have you seen the hotel?" asked Matilda.

"No, I haven't." replied Sue.

"Then you are in for a lovely time. What about Cleveland? Have you visited the sights?"

"The city looks so lovely, now. Let's go to the Flats when Mark comes."

"Oh, how nice, I'd like that." Sue felt happy for Matilda.

"If you need any help from us, don't be afraid to ask. I think I'll unpack now and you can show me your ring later." Sue went upstairs singing away. She was looking forward to a good time. Seeing young love always made her feel sentimental.

Twenty-Eight

An Important Decision

Mark had packed a small bag and moved into a furnished apartment, and knew he should have lived on his own after college. He knew plenty of other men his age that remained at home because of lack of finances for apartments. At the time, he saw nothing wrong in living with his parents, but with his mother constantly arguing over Matilda, he knew it was time to leave.

He had a bank account. By not having to pay rent, Mark had invested in good stocks and investments and could buy a decent home, but knew that he would not be able to maintain it. The hotel business had anti-social hours, and since the death of his sister, he practically lived there.

His mother had not accepted the fact that he was marrying Matilda. She spent her days nagging Mark to break off the engagement. She caused a rift that did not appear would mend. In no way, could she change his mind. This weekend, he was flying in to see Matilda to discuss their wedding.

Janet was upset that Mark had moved, and now sought his forgiveness. However, Mark was still angry. Eventually, he felt his mother would accept Matilda, but he knew his mother could be stubborn. On the other hand, his father was thrilled at having Matilda join their family, and Mark felt he could convince Janet that she was the right one.

Mark walked out of the Cleveland Airport after a bumpy flight, and was glad when the plane landed. Matilda greeted him. One look at her, and he knew he was doing the right thing. Her large brown eyes lifted his spirits.

"Matilda darling, let's get married right away."

"Oh Mark," she laughed, "the courthouse is all right with me, but the ballroom at Christmas is so romantic, and I know in my heart that is what you want. Anyway, we have to think of your family and mine. We have to plan."

"Matilda, you and your plans crack me up. Talking of plans, I've brought you a catalogue from the University of Miami, so you can look at the courses. It will be good to visit the campus. What am I saying? I don't want a wife smarter than me. I have to keep you in the kitchen."

"Oh, Mark, that was so sweet of you." Matilda kissed him passionately.

"Are you sure you don't want to get married this weekend?" Mark held her close.

Everyone greeted Mark with excitement. Richard congratulated him and shook his hand.

"I've made reservations at a restaurant in the flats to celebrate on Saturday night. My parents are here and want to join us."

"Wonderful," answered Mark.

"Mark, Matilda's ring is magnificent. You certainly have good taste," said Sue.

"You know Mark, Al and I had a brief engagement. I have had no regrets."

"Richard, where's the champagne?" Sue got up to find the crystal glasses.

"I have none. Tomorrow, we all celebrate with plenty of bubbles."

Twenty-Nine

Mrs. Wiggins

Carrie put down Matilda's letter. She read over the line. "Carrie, you just have to come here to be my bridesmaid."

Carrie did not know what to think. Most of all, she hoped Matilda hadn't lost her mind. "I'm no millionaire. How can I afford the airline tickets?" She decided to go and visit Mrs. Wiggins and talk over Matilda's wedding.

Carrie rang the bell several times and waited. She knew Mrs. Wiggins should be home from work by now. She looked up and saw Nifty on the window ledge looking out. A door opened in the flat next to Mrs. Wiggin's.

"Hello, there." A man of about forty-five came out. "Are you looking for Mrs. Wiggins?"

"Why yes, I am."

"Mm, are you a friend?" asked the neighbor.

"Yes, I am."

"Well, see here, her daughter came over here a while ago to take some things to the hospital. She got hurt at work."

"What? In which hospital is she?"

"It's the Ealing Hospital in Uxbridge Road."

"Right, thank you. What about the cat?"

"Mrs. Wiggins' daughter left me the key so I could feed the cat."

"Thanks a lot," said Carrie. "Oh, what's your name?" she asked.

"It's Josh Smith."

"Thanks so much for caring for Mrs. Wiggin's cat," said Carrie.

Carrie arrived at the hospital and gave her name and waited.

Emily Wiggins came over to Carrie and thanked her for coming.

"My mother has been burned by hot coffee spilled on her left leg. She has second degree burns. The doctor said she is going to be all right, but has to remain in hospital for a few days. Thanks for coming over, Carrie."

"Can I see her?" asked Carrie.

"Well, I suppose so. I think they have given her something to help with the pain. She is sort of dopey."

Both went to the hospital ward and sat by Anne Wiggin's bed-side. She managed a faint smile and closed her eyes. The two women talked quietly. Emily said as soon as her mother was able to leave the hospital she would be coming to her house to stay until she was fully recovered.

Emily and her husband Jim lived on the outskirts of London in a semi detached small house. Her brother Eric worked as an electrician and had his own flat, and remained a contented bachelor.

Emily had just telephoned Eric to let him know of his mother's accident. Emily looked at Carrie. "We have to ring Matilda and tell her." Both women stared at each other.

Finally, Emily said she did not have Matilda's phone number in America. "Tell you what; let me ring her. I'll give you the number when I get home. Meanwhile, I'll contact her tomorrow if you like."

"All right, Carrie. That would be lovely," answered Emily.

"I'll ring her around one in the afternoon. The time should be okay there. I won't let Matilda panic. I'll tell her what has happened and that you are going to care for her."

"I'm so tired and worried about Mum's recovery. Still, it's best to wait and see what the doctor has to say. I just can't believe this has happened. The manager phoned me at work to tell me they had sent her by cab to the closest hospital. I came here at once. I stayed a while, and then went to Mum's flat to feed the cat. She has a nice neighbor who said he will take care of it. Mr. Smith seems a decent bloke. I found the cat's food and gave it to him. You know how Mum feels about that cat!"

"I wondered how this could have happened. According to the report, a customer had his foot stuck out of the booth he was sitting in, and my mother tripped, and the coffee spilled over her left leg. She has always been very careful around the customers with hot food. So what can I say? It's an accident. I just hope and pray she recovers from this."

"Emily, of course she will. Your mother is strong." Carrie got closer to the bedside and held Mrs. Wiggins hand. She opened her eyes and smiled at Carrie and Emily.

Thirty

Carrie's Phone Call

Sue felt rested after a good night's sleep. She came down to breakfast early and decided to make pancakes for her grandchildren. She felt so happy to be with her family. She could give Matilda a little break, now. Sue decided to approach Richard to discuss it. She felt Matilda would need time to start making wedding preparations now that Mark was here.

Matilda came down to breakfast to a plate of pancakes. "Wow, am I being spoiled. Thank you, Sue." Matilda sparkled.

Al looked over at Joey. On his mind was hitting that ball and getting on the golf course. Mark came out of the family room and greeted everyone. "Something smells good."

"I've made a load of pancakes. Sit down and enjoy." Sue got the syrup and handed it to Mark.

"Well, Joey eat up, said Al. "We are going out to practice golf."

"Cool. Where's Dad?"

"So tell me, Matilda, where did my son go?" asked Al.

"He needs more exercise because of too much sitting at work, so he's started jogging early each morning. I don't think he's going to eat those delicious pancakes." She put out an extra plate just in case. Mark came over and planted a kiss on Matilda's cheek. Matilda smiled up at him.

"I'll clean up. Richard can eat something sensible, later," said Matilda. Sue approached the counter and squeezed some oranges while Jennie played with the dishes in the soapy water.

Richard opened the door feeling great after his morning run. "Well you two. Are you ready to go to the Flats tonight?"

"Absolutely," answered Mark.

Al got up. "Bye all, see you later," As far as Al was concerned, he wanted nothing to interfere with golf. All social plans he left to Sue.

"I need to straighten up the house a little. You two can decide on who's going to take a shower first," said Matilda to the children.

The phone rang and Richard answered. "Hello, is this the Evergreen residence?" Carrie asked.

"Yes, it is."

"I'm a friend of Matilda's. May I speak to her please?"

"Sure." Richard had a surprised look when he handed Matilda the phone. "Here, Matilda, the voice sounds English."

"Oh really, I wonder who's calling." Matilda heard Carrie's voice. "Hello Carrie. Guess you received my letter. Well, are you going to be my bridesmaid? You better say yes. I miss you something awful."

"Yes Matilda, I received it. When do you think you will be coming home?"

"I don't know." Mark is visiting and we are going to plan the wedding."

"The reason I rang was to tell you about your mum."

"What about Mum?"

"She had a slight accident and is in hospital with a burned leg." Carrie told Matilda all she knew. Matilda paused and said nothing.

"Matilda, are you there?"

Matilda felt her legs weaken. Just the mention of her mother being hurt sent her into a panic. "Carrie, I'll come home as quickly as I can. I will need to check the flights leaving from Cleveland Hopkins Airport."

"Matilda, I don't think it's necessary to come home, yet. Your mother is going to be fine. Emily will care for her when she comes out of the hospital."

"But Carrie, I need to see for myself what her condition is. I've been gone a long time and I miss her. I feel she needs me. I've been here almost two years and have saved my money for college and managed to put away some money for the fare home. It will be fine."

"Well, you are right about that. She does miss you. I've been going over once a week. We all miss you. You make the decision.

Meanwhile, I want you to know she has good care, and I'll ring you again with any more news on her condition."

Matilda caught her breath. "How bad is she?"

"Matilda, she is going to be fine. I just rang to let you know she is in hospital in the West End near where she works." Carrie gave Matilda all the information.

"Carrie, I will ring when I will arrive at Heathrow. There's no need to pick me up."

Mark looked at Matilda and saw the lights go out of her eyes. "What's wrong, darling?"

"Oh, Mark, it's my mother. I must go to her. She's had an accident, and she's is in hospital in London."

The family rallied around Matilda. "Don't worry, Matilda." Sue put her arm around her and comforted her. "I'm here and will take care of my grandchildren. You just do what you need to do. Seeing your mother is the right thing."

"It will be all right, darling. I'll help you. We'll celebrate later." Mark proceeded to comfort Matilda.

Thirty-One

The Arrangements

Matilda packed her clothes. She looked in the mirror and told herself not to cry in front of the children, but would remain confident. She loved them. These last weeks, she had seen Joey become a happy boy and Jennie look to her for her needs. She made sure the children would see her smile, and would reassure them that she was coming back soon. This she knew she must do with poise.

Joey brought Matilda's case down to the front door. The night before she sat with the children and explained she was leaving on a brief visit to England to visit her mother, and had shown Joey and Jennie a photograph of her.

Mark stayed and helped arrange her flight out of Cleveland on United Airlines. Matilda's car would remain at the Evergreen's. Mark decided to return to Miami and pick up his passport and then fly over to London to see Matilda's mother and family. His father said he could manage the hotel and was feeling all right.

The family waited for Matilda to board the plane that would depart to London and her mother. The children sat on the bench close to Matilda.

"Don't leave. Stay here with me." Joey began wailing, and hung on to Matilda. With that reaction, Jennie started crying when she saw her brother sobbing.

"Listen, Joey, I am going for a short while and I shall phone you from England." She knelt down and held the children close.

"When you return home, you will find a surprise under your pillows." Matilda had left a new children's story and coloring book for them. Inside the books was a written note that Richard could read to them. "I shall be back before you know it," said Matilda.

Sue Evergreen's eyes filled with tears which flowed like a faucet down her cheeks, and this time she was not concerned about her mascara smearing. She had always wanted a daughter, and had this been so, she would have wished for a girl like Matilda. "This girl really loves my grandchildren and they her," thought Sue.

It was time to leave. Passengers began boarding the plane. "See you soon, darling."

Mark held and kissed Matilda and said she looked like royalty in her pink hat. Matilda laughed and gave a little twirl. She was finally wearing her pink dress. The special day had come, and Matilda looked exquisite. This was not the day she would have chosen to wear it, but she knew the children would enjoy seeing her dressed up.

Sue looked up and wiped her red eyes to see Matilda smile and disappear from view. They waited to watch the plane lift up to a clear blue sky. As the plane climbed, the children clung to Richard by the airport window, where they witnessed the jet vanish into white clouds.

"I always knew that I selected the right nanny for my grandchildren. I knew it in my bones." Sue took Al's arm. He looked at his wife and knew what she was thinking.

"Come along, Sue, let's take our grandchildren home. We have lots to do today."

"Why, of course dear, I know we do." Sue took Joey and Jennie's hands and whisked them through the airport with Richard and Mark walking close behind.

Thirty-Two

Returning to London

"Well, Dad, I feel like a traveling salesman. These last few weeks all I am doing is flying."

"Do you have your ticket?" asked Ron.

"It's in my jacket pocket," answered Mark.

"Did you say good bye to your mother?"

"Of course, I did."

"Is everything all right?" asked Ron. "What did your mother have to say about Matilda? I believe she was upset because she felt you have only known her a short while, and you should wait to make sure."

"Dad, I've been all through this before. Mom and I are okay. She has accepted the fact that Matilda is going to become my wife and is looking forward to the wedding preparations. She and I talked it all out. Anyway, at my age, I should hope I know what is right for me. Matilda is the one. Do you understand, Dad? Just think of all those couples living together. That is not for us. Just get the hotel ballroom ready for a Christmas Eve wedding, and we'll be married by a judge. Check the calendar and clear it for us." Mark looked tentatively at his father.

"Mark, consider it done. That fiancé of yours just lights up my heart. How long is Matilda going to stay as a nanny with the Evergreens?"

"I believe she mentioned something about leaving at the end of August to register for classes at Miami University and stay at a dormitory there. I gave her the school's catalogue, so she can decide on her classes. She will be there until we marry. She told Richard her plans."

"Oh. So Matilda is going to be a student," said Ron.

"Yes, you have that right, Dad."

"You know, Mark, I wish that I had gone to college. I might have learned a thing or two."

"Dad, you are just fine the way you are."

"Mark that girl thrills my heart. What I need right now is a cigar."

"Dad that's what you don't need," replied Mark.

"Are you sure you will be in London for only two weeks? It's too bad about Mrs. Wiggins burning herself like that. Did Matilda mention how long the burn will take to heal?" inquired Ron.

"It will be a mess for two to three weeks. I'm hoping I can help them out," answered Mark.

"All right, call me as soon as you can. Mom and I send our best wishes to Matilda and her mother."

Ron was not happy at Mark leaving, but fortunately Jacob and Aaron were helping him, but he knew they did not have the caliber of Mark's talent for the business.

Matilda had spent her days nursing her mother and tending the wound on her leg from the recent burn. Matilda had phoned the Evergreens and chatted to Joey and Jennie. Both said they were drawing and coloring pictures for her. Matilda expected Mark's arrival any minute. Suddenly, there was a knock on the door.

"Oh, Mark, how wonderful that you are here," cried Matilda. Mark had taken a cab from Heathrow Airport directly to Mrs. Wiggins's flat.

"You have been out of my sight for too long, so I decided to put a stop to that," said Mark as he yawned and rubbed his eyes.

"Poor darling, I didn't come to meet you. You are amazing. Come on, I'll see that you get some rest," uttered Matilda.

Matilda went to Josh Smith's flat to ring Carrie to tell her Mark had arrived and to join them for breakfast. She then rang her sister Emily and brother, Eric, to arrange a time when they could meet Mark.

"So you're the man who has swept my daughter off her feet." Mrs. Wiggins embraced Mark, and looked at him from the top of his head to the bottom of his shoes.

"Well, I suppose you will have to do. Looks like Matilda has chosen well. Lord knows, it's a good thing, or I might ask you to leave."

Mrs. Wiggins let out a hearty laugh. "Welcome, Mark. I'm glad that you could come over, but not to see me in this silly mess. But I'm on the mend and getting about the flat. In another week or so, I'll return to work. My customers miss me, and I them. I guess they like my jokes," proclaimed Mrs. Wiggins.

She stayed on the couch resting her leg. A pile of old magazines were beside her along with an empty teacup. "I can't stand all this fussing about me. It's ridiculous. I'm not that bad." She had always been quite independent and liked it that way.

"Well, I've come to see you. How are you? How's that leg?" asked Mark.

"Not to worry, love. The doctor has to give it another look. Matilda did not have to carry on so much, but I am happy she came. Two years was a long time for her to be away, but that's what she wanted. Now she's told me she is going to get married in Miami Beach. That probably means she'll stay in America. It boggles my mind."

"Why don't we talk in the morning? You look as though you could use some rest. Eric's room is set up for you. Sorry, this is not Buckingham Palace, but Matilda has made it nice for you. She told me how big the houses are in the States. So love, hope you won't feel too cramped up."

Mark looked about the room and swallowed hard. "Poor Matilda," he thought. She certainly had no great material things, but she had everything else that was important to him.

Nifty appeared. He swung around Mark's legs and almost made him trip.

"Careful, we don't want you to fall. You get some sleep. Come here Nifty. There's a good cat," said Mrs. Wiggins picking him up.

"Carrie will be here in the morning and have breakfast with us. How are you two getting along?" asked Matilda.

Thirty-Three

Mrs. Wiggins' Flat

"Good morning. What's that smell?" asked Mark.

"It is kippers, love." Mrs. Wiggins had the breakfast table set and was busy turning the kippers over in the frying pan. "I'm cooking you an English breakfast. Come on, sit down. Get comfortable."

"You are supposed to be resting that leg," remarked Mark.

"I have for a fortnight. It's beginning to feel itchy. Besides, in another week I will be completely recovered, so there!"

"Matilda's mother is a good cook, and I just adore the way she cooks kippers," said Carrie who had arrived very early. "Where's Matilda?"

"Go see if she's awake, Carrie," said Mrs. Wiggins. Carrie left. Mrs. Wiggins sat by Mark. "Those two are going to chat for a while. Trust me. Matilda has told me all about you and the Evergreen children. It seems as though she's gotten quite attached to those little ones. I wish I could meet all of them."

"So you shall. I have brought tickets for you and Carrie to come to our wedding. It's a round trip on British Airways, so you had better get completely well," replied Mark. "We can't get married without your presence and Carrie as our bridesmaid."

"Oh my," she uttered. She hobbled into the bedroom to tell Carrie and Matilda the news. The two shrieked with joy. "And look, we are going to stay at the Skylight Inn." Mrs. Wiggins fell on the bed. The three women hugged each other while Mark calmly ate his kippers.

"Well you three, are you going to eat breakfast with me?" he called out. Matilda rushed into Mark's arms. The four ate and drank large cups of strong tea. Mark asked to find a phone so he could call his father.

"Matilda will take you to our neighbor. Josh Smith is a good bloke. He let's us use his phone," replied Mrs. Wiggins. "I'll invite him up for a nice cup of tea and a large helping of homemade trifle. It's his favorite. No doubt, he would enjoy meeting you, Mark. He's been ever so good to me." She gave Mark a broad smile and a devilish wink.

"How long will it take to get a phone installed here?" asked Mark.

"Why, I have no idea."

"I shall see that you have a phone before I return to the States," said Mark.

Mrs. Wiggins gasped. "Don't be daft, Mark, I'm used to living without one," she answered.

"Matilda will need to call you often and let you know what she's up to."

"Don't worry, I'll handle it," said Mark.

"Oh, my lord," quailed Mrs. Wiggins.

Thirty-Four

The Wedding Discussion

"Hello, Richard. How are Joey and Jennie?"

"Matilda, it's great to hear your voice. The children are fine. My mother is keeping them occupied, but they certainly are missing you. How is your mother?" asked Richard.

"Her leg is healing nicely, and I shall return in another week. Mark and I have planned our wedding at the Skylight Inn on Christmas Eve and would like the children to be ring bearers. Will that be all right with you? Carrie, my long time friend will be a bridesmaid. She is a lovely person. I'm sending pictures of all of us, so you can see for yourself."

"Matilda are you trying to do match making?" joked Richard.

"Well, I hadn't thought of that, but she will make a fine dancing partner for you. What do you think, Richard?"

"Matilda, it will be my pleasure to accompany Carrie, providing I like her picture."

"Oh Richard, you will, you will." answered Matilda. She could hear his laughter as she hung up the phone. Matilda thanked Mr. Smith for the use of the phone and paid him for the call. She and Mark decided to take a walk. "How are Richard and the children?" asked Mark.

"They seem fine," answered Matilda.

"That's good," replied Mark.

Mark took Matilda's hand and strolled with her down London's busy streets. They glanced in the shop windows. "How about it if I shop for a wedding dress while I am here? Carrie can help select it, and perhaps find her bridesmaid dress. And my mother, don't you think she will look pretty in blue? And of course, Carrie will be in pink." Matilda became exuberant.

"Oh, no, don't drag me into this, Matilda. Let's elope. It would be so much easier."

"Impossible darling, it's the gorgeous ballroom at the Skylight Inn that is waiting for us and a big band playing with Sue Evergreen singing. What could be better? Nothing else will do."

"All right, Matilda. You win," answered Mark.

Matilda thought about the English Nanny School and how much she had learned there. She opened her purse.

"What are you doing?" asked Mark.

"I'm writing some reminders in my journal. I need to thank Joey's teacher, Mrs. Adams, for helping me with him. I must contact her when we return to the United States."

"Matilda you amaze me! Is there anything else that concerns you?"

"I can't think of anything else right now."

"That's good. Come on Matilda. Let's enjoy London while we can."

CPSIA information can be obtained at www.ICGtesting.com
Printed in the USA
LVOW08s0337041113

359783LV00002B/66/P